THE ROOTS OF ETERNITY

THE AWAKENING

KAVISH TOLANI
TAMANAA TOLANI

To those who dare to believe in the extraordinary, who see magic hidden in the ordinary, and who find adventure in the quietest of places—this book is for you.

To our family, whose love and encouragement has been our foundation. Your unwavering support has given us the strength to create, to dream, and to bring this world to life. Every word on these pages carries a piece of your kindness, patience, and belief in me.

To our friends, the ones who have walked beside us through every twist and turn, who have listened to our ideas, debated about our characters, and shared in our excitement—your inspiration has made this journey all the more meaningful.

To the readers, stepping into this world for the first time—may you find wonder, adventure, and courage within these pages. May the mysteries beneath the roots of this story spark your imagination and remind you that every legend begins with a single step into the unknown.

To the storytellers who have come before and those yet to come—your words have shaped countless worlds, and this our my humble addition to the vast and boundless universe of stories.

And finally, to those who seek light even in the darkest of places, who fight for what is right, and who believe in the power of hope—this story belongs to you.

This is just the beginning. The journey awaits.

Contents

FOREWORD

Stories have the power to take us beyond the limits of our world, to places where the impossible becomes real. This book is one such journey—one that delves into mystery, adventure, and the battle between light and darkness. At its heart, it is a tale of friendship, courage, and the choices that define us.

When we first imagined this world, it was just a spark—an idea of a hidden force beneath the roots of an ancient tree, waiting to be discovered. That spark grew, and soon, the characters came to life: Ethan, the genius whose mind merges with technology; Tara, whose designs shape reality; Jax, the warrior with unbreakable strength; Nina, an artist bound to nature itself. Their destinies intertwine with Oakheart, the guardian of a secret that could change everything.

But every great story needs a challenge, an obstacle to overcome. That's where Ravok enters—a force of destruction seeking to undo the very balance of life.With deception lurking in the shadows and unexpected allies among enemies, the journey becomes more than just a battle—it becomes a test of trust, sacrifice, and truth.

As you turn these pages, we invite you to lose yourself in this world, to walk alongside the heroes as they uncover their powers, face impossible odds, and discover the strength that lies within.

This is just the beginning of a much larger tale, and we hope it stays with you long after the final page.So step forward, dive into the unknown,and remember—sometimes, the greatest stories are hidden beneath the roots.

PREFACE

Every story begins with a question. For us, it was this: What if an ancient force, hidden beneath the earth, held the power to shape the fate of the world? From that question, this book was born—a tale of adventure, mystery, and the battle between creation and destruction.

The journey of writing this book has been both thrilling and challenging. As the characters took shape, so did their struggles, their strengths, and their destinies. Ethan, a genius whose mind is evolving beyond human limits; Tara, a designer whose art comes to life; Jax, a warrior bound by strength and loyalty; and Nina, an artist who becomes one with nature's magic. Each of them was crafted to explore not just power, but the responsibility that comes with it.

At the heart of this story lies the Tree of Life, a source of immeasurable energy, protected for centuries. But every great force has its counterpart, and Ravok, the immortal antagonist, seeks to claim it for himself. The journey these heroes undertake is not just about defeating an enemy—it's about discovering their purpose, facing their fears, and understanding the cost of true power.

This book is a blend of science, fantasy, and the timeless theme of unity. It is about trust, betrayal, and the choices that shape our destiny.

We hope that as you read, you will not just follow the story but experience the journey—one filled with challenges, revelations, and the thrill of the unknown.

Welcome to a world hidden beneath the roots. The adventure awaits.

Acknowledgements

First and foremost, We want to express my deepest gratitude to my parents (**Jeetandra Tolani & Dr.Aarti Deenadayal Tolani**). Your unwavering support, encouragement, and love have been the foundation of everything we do. You have always believed in us, even when we doubted ourselves, and for that, we are forever grateful. Your guidance has shaped us into the people we are today, and this book would not have been possible without your constant motivation.

To our grandparents(**Dr.D.S Deenadayal,Dr. Mamata Deenadayal & Meena Tolani**), your wisdom, kindness, and stories have inspired us in ways we cannot put into words. The values you have instilled in us—the importance of perseverance, honesty, and hard work—are reflected in every page of this book. Thank you for always being there, for sharing your experiences, and for reminding us that stories have the power to connect generations.

To our Uncles and Aunts (**Aditya Deenadayal , Arjun Deenadayal , Ankita Deenadayal , Anupama Mettler & Jaya Sangtani**) who taught us confidence,resilience and to follow our dreams without inhibitions.

This book is dedicated to you, with all our love and appreciation.

Prologue

Deep beneath the earth, hidden within an ancient forest untouched by time, the roots of the Tree of Life pulsed with a quiet, steady glow. The light within them was not just energy—it was existence itself. Every breath of wind, every ripple in the water, every heartbeat in the world above was connected to it. But not all who sought the Tree wished to protect it.

A shadow moved through the darkness, its presence sending a tremor through the ground. Ravok, the immortal one, stood before the roots, his crimson eyes reflecting the glow of the sacred tree. He had searched for centuries, seeking the one thing that could break the balance of life itself. And now, he was close.Behind him, his most trusted follower, Leo, remained silent, his gaze fixed on the ancient trunk. Ravok turned to him, his voice cold yet filled with purpose.

"The time is near. The guardians grow weaker. Soon, the Heartstone will be mine."Leo nodded, but something flickered in his eyes. A hesitation. A doubt. But he did not speak.

Far from the forest, in the bustling world above, four lives continued unknowingly, their destinies about to change forever. Ethan, a mind beyond human understanding. Tara, an artist whose creativity held untapped power. Jax, strong and unshaken. Nina, connected to the world in ways she had yet to realize.They had no idea that soon, they would be called upon. That their lives would be rewritten by forces older than time itself.

Our Website

For readers who wish to explore the world of The Roots of Eternity beyond the final page, we've created a special corner of the internet just for you. Visit our official website to find bonus content, character secrets, early sketches, and hidden lore. To unlock the release date for future content use the password: heartstone.5 — a name that holds the power of this entire journey. Only those who have walked beside the protectors will truly understand its meaning. This is our way of saying thank you—and letting the adventure grow in new ways, even after the last word.

Explore the Roots on : therootsofeternty.com

About Us

The Sibling Collaboration :

We are Kavish and Tamanaa, two siblings with different passions but a shared love for storytelling. Our journey began with a curious glance out of the window, sparking a creative collaboration that has become more than we ever imagined.

I Kavish, was driven by a fascination with science and reality, crafting the logical backbone of our narratives. Tamanaa , on the other hand, could easily dive into the world of imagination, designing characters and weaving fantastic elements that brought our stories to life.

Our collaboration taught us the power of combining our unique strengths. Where there were once sibling quarrels, there's now synergy, turning differences into creative fuel.

Together, we've created a world where imagination meets reality, inspiring others to embrace the beauty of teamwork.

This book is our testament to the magic that unfolds when diverse talents unite. We hope our journey encourages others to dream, create, and collaborate with those they cherish.

Kavish Tolani

Kavish Tolani, a spirited 15-year-old, is currently a 10th-grade student at Indus Universal School in Hyderabad. Known for his exceptional problem-solving skills, Kavish passionately engages in various interests. He is a chess enthusiast and plays the guitar, bringing joy to his mother. Celebrated as an Olympiad champion at his school, Kavish also finds great pleasure in exploring the realms of mathematics, physics, chemistry, computers, and coding. Demonstrating remarkable leadership, he served as a house captain, guiding his peers with dedication. Kavish has creatively designed websites for his family and aspires to join a business school, aiming to make a positive societal impact through entrepreneurship, job creation, and becoming a business tycoon.

Tamanaa Tolani

Tamanaa Tolani, at 12, is Kavish's talented younger sister and a seventh grader at Indus Universal School in Secunderabad. Known for her boundless creativity, Tamanaa excels as an artist, using her free time to paint and design book characters. Her vivid imagination has significantly contributed to the sibling collaboration on this book. A loving friend and cherished daughter, she is her parent's pride and joy. Passionate about storytelling, Tamanaa enjoys reading books, watching television, and diving into anime worlds. She aspires to pursue a career in the creative field, driven by her desire to bring imagination to life through artistic endeavors.

I

A Strange Beginning

Ethan sat quietly at his desk, the glow of his computer screen reflecting on his glasses. The office was buzzing with activity, but to Ethan, it all felt distant. He was in his own world, his mind deep in the complex lines of code he was working on. As a manager at the software company, he was used to handling difficult tasks. The world of technology and logic was where he felt most comfortable.

"Ethan, you still working on that update?" came a voice from beside him.Ethan looked up to see Jax, leaning casually against his desk. Jax was his best friend at work, but the two were very different. Ethan was all about precision and focus, while Jax was more carefree, always joking and keeping things light."If you can call it 'working,'" Ethan replied with a small smirk. "I'm fixing bugs from last week's update. But hey, it's a living."Jax grinned, taking a seat on the edge of Ethan's desk.

"Man, you need to take a break. You're going to fry your

brain if you keep staring at that screen all day."I'm fine," Ethan said, returning his attention to the screen. "Besides, I'm almost done with this part."Jax picked up a piece of paper from the desk and started folding it into a paper airplane. "You know, you could be a little more... human. I'm sure the world won't end if you step away from the keyboard for five minutes."Ethan rolled his eyes but couldn't help but chuckle. "That's rich coming from you. The guy who spends more time making jokes than doing actual work."Jax threw the paper airplane at Ethan's head. "Hey, I'm multitasking! You should try it sometime."Ethan just shook his head, his fingers still moving over the keyboard. He and Jax had been working together for years, and their friendship had become one of the few things that made the daily grind bearable. Where Ethan was focused and logical, Jax kept things light and entertaining.

Just then, the office door opened, and a man stepped inside. He was tall, dressed in a long, dark coat, and wore a wide-brimmed hat that shadowed his face. He seemed out of place in the busy office. His presence made Ethan pause for a second. He didn't know the man, and there was something odd about the way he moved—like he was observing everyone without being noticed."Who's that?" Jax whispered, his eyes following the man.Ethan squinted, but the man quickly disappeared into the crowd of employees.

"I have no idea. Maybe a client?"

"Maybe," Jax said, but he didn't look convinced.

"He was... weird. Something about him felt off."Ethan didn't respond, but he couldn't shake the feeling that Jax was right. There was something strange about the man.Later that afternoon, Tara stood in the middle of her boutique, adjusting a display of clothes. The sun streamed through the large windows, casting a warm glow over the room. Tara loved this part of her job. She was a designer, and her store was her passion. Each piece of clothing, every scarf and dress, was her creation. She enjoyed the peace and quiet of the shop, especially when she had time to think.

Her coworker, Nina, was folding some shirts nearby. They had worked together for years, and Tara trusted her opinion on just about everything."Hey, Nina, what do you think of this display?" Tara asked, stepping back to admire the clothes.Nina looked over and smiled. "It looks great! That scarf you designed is beautiful. It really stands out."Tara smiled at the compliment. "Thanks! I was thinking of adding some new colors next week, maybe something bold."You should!" Nina agreed. "People will love it. You've got a real talent for design."Tara felt a small sense of pride, but her thoughts were interrupted when she glanced out the window. Across the street, she noticed a man standing in the shadows. He was tall, wearing a dark coat, and had a wide-brimmed hat. His face was hard to see, but Tara could tell he was watching her store. She felt a sudden unease."Nina," Tara said, her voice barely above a whisper. "Do you see that guy out there?"Nina followed her gaze and frowned. "Yeah, I see him. He's just standing there,staring at the window. It's kind of creepy."Tara nodded, feeling her heartbeat quicken. "Something's not right about him. He's been there for a while."Before they could discuss it further, a bus passed by, briefly blocking their view of the street. When the bus was gone, the man was no longer standing there.

Tara let out a breath she didn't realize she had been holding."Did he just... disappear?" Tara asked, still staring at the empty street.Nina shrugged, trying to calm Tara. "Maybe he just walked off. Let's not overthink it."But Tara couldn't shake the feeling that something was wrong. She turned to Nina. "I don't know. It just didn't feel normal.

"Later that evening, Ethan and Jax were in Ethan's apartment, eating takeout and watching TV. It had been a long day, and Jax was more than happy to relax. But Ethan couldn't stop thinking about the man from earlier. There was something about him that bothered him, something he couldn't quite place."You still thinking about that guy?" Jax asked, noticing the serious look on Ethan's face."I can't help it," Ethan replied, running a hand through his hair. "I saw him again, after work. Right outside the office."

Jax looked over at him, his expression shifting from playful to concerned. "You think he's following you?"Ethan shrugged. "Maybe. But why? It's not like I'm anyone important."

"Well, you never know," Jax said with a half-smile. "But if it makes you feel better, I'll go out with you tomorrow. We can check it out together."Ethan appreciated the gesture but didn't feel any better. "Maybe we're just overthinking it. I don't know."

"Alright, alright," Jax said, raising his hands in surrender. "Let's drop it for now. We've got pizza, and we're not gonna solve this mystery tonight."Ethan smiled faintly, but he couldn't shake the feeling that the man was more than just a strange passerby. And just like that, the thought of the man lingered in his mind as the evening wore on.

Tara was sitting on her couch, her phone in her hands. She had spent the whole evening trying to distract herself, but the man kept appearing in her thoughts. She was sure he had been watching her store. She tried to focus on the TV, but the unease gnawed at her.

She picked up the phone and called Nina. "Nina, I keep thinking about that guy.I don't know why, but I feel like he's been following me."Nina's voice came through clearly.

"You're probably just being paranoid. I'm sure it's nothing. But if it makes you feel better, let's keep an eye out. If you see him again, we'll figure it out."Tara felt a little better. "Yeah, maybe you're right. I'll try not to worry about it."
She hung up, but the feeling didn't go away. There was something about the man that didn't sit right with her. She couldn't explain it, but she had a sense that something big was about to happen.

Later that night, the man in the long coat stood on a rooftop overlooking the city.
He was still, like a shadow in the night. His eyes were fixed on the buildings below, scanning the streets as if waiting for something—or someone."It's time," he whispered to himself. "They will come together soon. I've watched them long enough."He turned away from the edge of the rooftop, disappearing into the darkness, his mission far from over.The next day, the lives of Ethan, Jax, Tara, and Nina would begin to change. They had no idea, but the mysterious man's plan was already set in motion.

The ordinary world they knew was about to collide with something much bigger, something powerful and dangerous and all of it would lead them to the Tree of Life.

II

The Mysterious Visitor

The next day, Ethan woke up early. The sun was just starting to rise, casting a soft orange glow over the city. He rubbed his eyes, feeling a little tired but determined to keep going. He had a strange feeling in his gut ever since the man in the coat had appeared. The thought of that mysterious figure made him uneasy.

"Ethan, you up yet?" Jax's voice came through the open bedroom door.

Ethan got out of bed and walked toward the door. "Yeah, just woke up. What's up?"

Jax stood in the hallway, holding a cup of coffee in one hand and his phone in the other. "We should grab some breakfast. I've got a weird feeling about today. You know, with that guy from yesterday."

Ethan nodded, still thinking about the strange man. "Yeah, I feel it too. Let's go."

The two of them went down to the café near Ethan's apartment. It was quite early in the morning, just a few customers sipping coffee and reading newspapers. They sat by the window, the warm light from outside filling the space.

"So, what do you think about all this?" Jax asked, looking out the window. "Is it just some coincidence or are we being watched?"

Ethan stirred his coffee slowly. "I don't know. But I've got this feeling that there's more to it. Maybe it's nothing, but I keep thinking about it."

Jax raised an eyebrow. "You're not usually the 'paranoid' type, Ethan. Maybe we should just forget about it. We've got enough to worry about with work and everything else."

Ethan sighed, looking out the window too. "Yeah, maybe you're right. But something about yesterday's meeting keeps bothering me. That man seemed... out of place. Like he was waiting for something."

"Maybe you're just overthinking," Jax said with a shrug. "Anyway, let's enjoy our breakfast."

They ate their food in silence for a few moments. But Ethan couldn't shake the feeling. As soon as they finished, they decided to head to the office. Work was a good distraction, he thought. It would keep his mind off the mysterious man.

Meanwhile, Tara and Nina were having a similar conversation. Tara had hardly slept the night before, turning over the events in her mind. Her store had been quiet in the morning, just the way she liked it, but the unease she felt was hard to ignore.

Nina noticed her distracted expression as she entered the store.

"Tara, you okay?" Nina asked, setting down a bag of fabric she had brought in.

Tara didn't answer right away, but instead went to the window, staring out at the street. "I don't know. I keep thinking about that guy from yesterday. The one who was standing outside the store."

Nina joined her at the window. "The one in the long coat and hat? Yeah, that was definitely creepy. What about him?"

"I don't know... I just have this feeling that he's still watching me," Tara said softly, her voice full of doubt. "I don't know why, but I can't shake the feeling that he's waiting for something."

Nina put a hand on Tara's shoulder, offering her comfort. "It's probably nothing, Tara. Maybe he was just a random person. There's always someone walking by."

Tara nodded, but she wasn't convinced. "Yeah, maybe."

Just then, the door of the store opened, and a woman walked in. Tara greeted her with a smile, but her mind was still far away, thinking about the man.

The day passed by slowly. Tara kept glancing at the window, expecting to see the man again, but he didn't appear. Yet, the feeling that something was wrong didn't go away.

Back at the office, Ethan couldn't focus on his work. His mind kept drifting back to the strange events of the past day. He kept thinking about the man with the hat and coat, and how he had seemed to be watching him. Jax noticed his distracted state and leaned over.

"You still thinking about that guy?" Jax asked, his voice low.

Ethan nodded slowly. "I can't help it. It feels like something big is coming, and I don't know what it is. It feels like... like we're being pulled into something."

Jax looked at Ethan with a raised eyebrow. "You've been watching too many action movies, my friend. Maybe we're just being paranoid. It could just be a coincidence."

"I don't know," Ethan replied. "I have this gut feeling that something's going to happen. We need to stay alert."

Jax leaned back in his chair, stretching his arms. "Alright, Mr. Detective, let's just keep our eyes open. But don't go overboard. We're just normal guys, remember?"

Ethan couldn't shake the unease, but he decided to let it go for now. He had a job to do, and he couldn't let his thoughts get in the way.

Later that evening, Tara decided to head home early. The day had been long, and she was feeling drained. As she walked through the streets, she glanced over her shoulder, half-expecting to see the man from the day before. But he was nowhere in sight.

As she walked into her apartment, she felt a slight sense of relief. At least she could relax for a bit. She changed into comfortable clothes and made herself some tea. But the feeling of being watched stayed with her.

Suddenly, there was a knock at her door. She jumped, startled. Her heart raced as she approached the door.

"Who is it?" she asked, her voice shaking slightly.

It was Nina. Tara opened the door quickly. "Nina, you scared me! What are you doing here?"

"I couldn't stop thinking about you," Nina said, her face full of concern. "I just wanted to check on you. You seemed pretty freaked out earlier today."

Tara smiled weakly. "Thanks, Nina. I appreciate it. It's just... I keep thinking about that man. I don't know why. Something feels wrong."

Nina stepped inside and sat down on the couch. "I know you're worried, but I'm sure it's just your imagination.

Maybe you're stressed from work or something."

Tara sat down next to her. "Maybe. But I've never felt this way before. It's like something is about to happen. I just don't know what."

Back at Ethan's apartment, he and Jax were talking again. Jax was trying to convince Ethan that he was overthinking things, but it wasn't working.

"I'm telling you, something is wrong," Ethan said. "I keep thinking that man is connected to something... something big."

Jax sighed. "Alright, alright. But I still think you're overreacting. Let's just drop it for now. We'll focus on work, and if anything weird happens again, we'll deal with it then."

Ethan wasn't so sure. But he agreed, reluctantly.

That night, as he lay in bed, he stared at the ceiling. The unease kept gnawing at him, and the thought of the mysterious man haunted him. He couldn't explain it, but he knew one thing for sure—things were about to change.

The next morning, Ethan got a strange call. It wasn't from work or a friend. It was from an unknown number. He hesitated before answering.

"Hello?" he asked.

A deep voice spoke on the other end. "Ethan, I need to see you. It's important. Meet me at the park. 3 p.m."

The line went dead before Ethan could respond. His heart pounded in his chest. He looked at Jax, who was sitting on the couch, playing a video game.

"Jax," Ethan said, his voice serious. "I think it's time we find out what's going on."

Jax turned to him, sensing the change in Ethan's tone. "What happened?"

Ethan showed him the phone. "We need to meet someone. I think we've been chosen for something."

Jax stood up, putting his game down. "Alright, let's go. This is getting interesting."

The park was empty when they arrived, except for a man standing in the shadows. Ethan's heart raced as he recognized him—the same man from the day before. The man in the long coat and wide-brimmed hat.

This time, Ethan wasn't afraid. He was ready to find out what this man wanted.

The man stepped forward. "Ethan, Jax. It's time for you to meet the others. We have much to discuss."

III

A New Team

Ethan and Jax followed the mysterious man into the park. The air was cool, and the shadows of the tall trees seemed to dance in the faint light of the setting sun. Ethan's heart raced. He had so many questions but decided to stay quiet for now. The man walked confidently, his long coat swaying as he moved. Jax kept glancing at Ethan, as if trying to figure out what he was thinking.

Finally, the man stopped near a large oak tree. He turned to face them, his dark eyes scanning their faces.

"Ethan, Jax," the man said, his voice deep and calm. "You are not alone. There are others like you, chosen for something bigger than yourselves."

"Chosen?" Ethan asked, his brows furrowed. "What are you talking about? Who are you?"

The man smiled slightly but didn't answer directly. "Follow me. You'll understand soon."

Ethan and Jax exchanged a look, unsure of what to do. But curiosity won over caution, and they followed the man deeper into the park. After a few minutes of walking, they saw two women standing by a bench. Ethan recognized them immediately—it was Tara and Nina.

"Tara? Nina?" Ethan called out, surprised.

The women turned toward him, their faces showing equal shock. Tara stepped forward. "Ethan? What are you doing here?"

Jax gave a small wave. "Looks like we're not the only ones pulled into this strange situation."

The man gestured for everyone to sit on the bench. "All of you were chosen for a reason. You are connected in ways you do not yet understand."

Tara crossed her arms, looking skeptical. "Who are you, and why do you keep saying we're chosen? Chosen for what?"

The man took a deep breath. "My name is Oakheart. That is all you need to know for now. I have brought you together because you are important. Together, you will face something far greater than anything you've ever known."

Nina frowned. "This sounds like something out of a movie. Why us? We're just regular people."

Oakheart shook his head. "You are not regular. You are special. Each of you hava a gift, though you may not know it yet. These gifts will awaken when the time is right. But first, you must learn to work together."

Ethan leaned forward, his curiosity growing. "Work together for what? What are we supposed to do?"

Oakheart looked at him seriously. "Protect the Tree of Life."

The First Test

Before anyone could ask more questions, Oakheart raised his hand. A sudden gust of wind blew through the park, and the surroundings began to change. The trees grew taller, their leaves turning dark green. The ground beneath them became softer, like moss. It felt like they had stepped into another world.

"What's happening?" Tara whispered, her voice trembling.

"This is your first test," Oakheart said. "I need to see if you can work together."

Before anyone could react, strange creatures began to appear from the shadows. They were small but fierce, with glowing red eyes and sharp claws. They looked like a mix between wolves and shadows.

"Fight them," Oakheart commanded. "But remember, you must rely on each other."

Ethan and Jax immediately stepped forward, trying to shield Tara and Nina. "Stay behind us," Jax said, his voice firm.

One of the shadow creatures lunged at them. Jax reacted quickly, punching it hard. The creature dissolved into black mist. Ethan grabbed a nearby stick and swung it at another creature, keeping it away from Tara.

Nina, however, wasn't content to just stand back. She grabbed a rock from the ground and threw it at one of the creatures. "I'm not going to just watch!" she said.

Tara hesitated, unsure of what to do. She had never been in a fight before. But when one of the creatures charged at her, something inside her shifted. She grabbed a long branch and held it out, keeping the creature at bay.

Ethan noticed her courage and smiled. "Nice move, Tara! Keep it up!"

The group slowly began to work together. Jax used his strength to knock the creatures away, while Ethan focused on keeping everyone organized. Nina was quick and clever, finding ways to distract the creatures, and Tara used her sharp instincts to defend herself and the others.

After what felt like hours, the last of the shadow creatures disappeared. Everyone was breathing heavily, their bodies tired but their spirits high.

Oakheart stepped forward, clapping his hands once. "You did well. You are not perfect yet, but you showed potential. This is just the beginning."

A Difficult Conversation

As the world around them returned to normal, the group sat on the bench again, exhausted. Tara was the first to speak.

"What was that?" she asked, her voice shaky. "Those creatures... they weren't normal."

Oakheart nodded. "They were shadows, creations of darkness. They are nothing compared to what you will face in the future."

Ethan wiped the sweat from his forehead. "This is insane. You're saying we're supposed to fight things like that? Why us? Why not someone else?"

Oakheart's expression softened. "Because the Tree of Life chose you. The tree is the source of all light and life in this world. Without it, everything will fall into darkness. There is a great evil that wants to destroy it. You must stop him."

Nina leaned forward, her eyes wide. "Who is this great evil?"

Oakheart's face darkened. "His name is Ravok. He is a demon, immortal and powerful. He will stop at nothing to destroy the Tree of Life and bring chaos to the world."

Jax crossed his arms. "And you expect us to fight this guy? We barely made it through those shadow creatures."

"You will grow stronger," Oakheart said firmly. "Each of you has a power inside you. It will awaken in time. But first, you must trust each other and learn to work as a team."

Tara still looked doubtful. "How can we trust each other? We just met."

Oakheart smiled slightly. "Trust is built through trials. This was just the first. There will be many more."

A Glimpse of Power

As the group prepared to leave, Oakheart stopped them. "Before you go, I must show you something."

He raised his hand, and a small orb of light appeared in the air. It floated toward each of them, pausing for a moment before moving to the next person.

When the light touched Ethan, he felt a strange warmth in his chest. Images flashed in his mind—machines, codes, and endless streams of data. He felt smarter, sharper, like he could solve any problem in the world.

When the light touched Tara, she felt a surge of creativity. She saw images of beautiful designs, colors, and shapes coming to life. It was as if her drawings could leap off the page and become real.

Jax felt a wave of strength wash over him when the light touched him. He saw himself running faster, jumping higher, and lifting heavy objects with ease. It was a power he had never imagined.

For Nina, the light brought a sense of transformation. She felt her body change, as if she could take on any form she wanted. It was both strange and exciting.

When the light faded, Oakheart looked at them with pride. "These are the seeds of your powers. They will grow stronger with time and training."

Ethan stared at his hands, still feeling the warmth of the light. "This... this is real, isn't it?"

"Yes," Oakheart said. "And it is only the beginning."

The Journey Begins

As the group left the park, they felt a mix of emotions—fear, excitement, and curiosity. They still didn't fully understand what was happening, but they knew one thing: their lives had changed forever.

Ethan walked beside Jax, deep in thought. "Do you think we can really do this?"

Jax shrugged. "I don't know. But we don't have much of a choice, do we?"

Tara and Nina walked a little behind them, talking quietly. Tara still had doubts, but Nina seemed more confident now.

"We'll figure it out," Nina said. "Together."

Ethan glanced back at them and nodded. He didn't know what the future held, but he was starting to believe that, maybe, they could handle it—if they worked as a team.

In the distance, Oakheart watched them leave. A faint smile crossed his face. He knew the road ahead would be hard, but he believed in them. They were the chosen ones, and their journey had just begun.

IV
Training for the Mission

The sun rose slowly, casting its golden light over the city. Ethan, Jax, Tara, and Nina found themselves standing in front of an old, abandoned warehouse. Oakheart had told them to meet here for their first training session. Ethan adjusted his glasses and looked at the others, still trying to process everything that had happened the day before.

"Does this place look... safe to you?" Tara asked, wrinkling her nose as she looked at the rusty metal door.

"I doubt 'safe' is on Oakheart's list of priorities," Jax said with a smirk. He stepped forward and pushed the door open. It creaked loudly, revealing a large empty space inside.

The group walked in cautiously. The room was dimly lit, with only a few rays of sunlight streaming through the cracks in the roof. Oakheart stood in the middle of the warehouse, his tall figure cloaked in shadows.

"Good. You're here," he said in his deep voice. "Today, we begin your training."

"Training for what, exactly?" Nina asked, crossing her arms.

Oakheart smiled slightly. "To protect the Tree of Life and defeat Ravok. But before you can do that, you must learn to use your powers and work as a team."

Discovering Strengths

Oakheart gestured to the far end of the warehouse. Four strange objects appeared out of nowhere. Ethan saw a glowing cube, Tara noticed a blank canvas, Jax spotted a large metal weight, and Nina saw a mirror.

"These are tools to awaken your powers," Oakheart explained. "Each one is connected to you in a unique way. Step forward and see what happens."

Ethan hesitated but decided to go first. He approached the glowing cube and touched it. Immediately, his mind was flooded with streams of data. He saw complex codes, equations, and blueprints flashing before his eyes.

"What's happening?" Ethan asked, his voice shaking.

"You're seeing the world as only you can," Oakheart said. "Your mind is like a supercomputer. You can solve problems faster than anyone else and build things beyond imagination. Trust your instincts."

Ethan nodded slowly, starting to feel more confident.

Next, Tara stepped up to the blank canvas. She hesitated, then picked up a nearby brush. As soon as the brush touched the canvas, vibrant colors burst to life. A tree appeared, its leaves shimmering with golden light. Suddenly, the tree leaped off the canvas and stood in front of her, real and alive.

Tara gasped. "Did I just... create that?"

Oakheart nodded. "Your designs can come to life. You can shape the world around you with your creativity."

Jax was next. He grabbed the metal weight and lifted it easily with one hand. Then, without warning, the weight began to grow heavier and heavier. Sweat dripped down Jax's face, but he held on. Finally, the weight stopped growing, and Jax tossed it aside.

"You have incredible strength," Oakheart said. "But your greatest power is your determination. Never give up, and you'll be unstoppable."

Finally, Nina stood in front of the mirror. She looked at her reflection nervously. Then, the image in the mirror began to shift. Her reflection changed into a bird, then a wolf, then a shadowy figure. Nina stepped back, startled.

"You are a shapeshifter," Oakheart said. "You can become anything you wish. But it will take practice to master your transformations."

Team Challenges

After everyone discovered their powers, Oakheart led them to the center of the warehouse. There, a large circular platform rose from the ground.

"This is where you will train together," Oakheart said. "The first step to protecting the Tree of Life is learning to work as a team."

The group stepped onto the platform, unsure of what to expect. Suddenly, the room around them transformed. They found themselves in a dense forest, surrounded by towering trees and thick bushes.

"What's going on?" Tara asked

"This is a simulation," Oakheart explained. His voice echoed around them, though he was no longer visible. "Your task is to find the golden key hidden in this forest. But beware—there are obstacles in your path."

Before anyone could ask questions, a loud roar echoed through the forest. Ethan's eyes widened. "What was that?"

"I think we're about to find out," Jax said, stepping forward and scanning the area.

A large creature emerged from the shadows. It looked like a bear, but its eyes glowed red, and its fur seemed to shimmer like metal. The group froze for a moment, unsure of what to do.

"Spread out!" Ethan shouted, taking charge. "We need a plan!"

Jax ran toward the creature, using his strength to wrestle it away from the others. Tara climbed up a nearby tree to get a better view of the forest. Nina transformed into a bird and flew above the creature, distracting it.

Meanwhile, Ethan studied the creature carefully. "It's not real," he muttered to himself. "It's a simulation. There has to be a weakness."

He noticed a glowing mark on the creature's chest. "Jax! Aim for its chest!"

Jax nodded and punched the glowing spot with all his strength. The creature roared one last time before disappearing into thin air.

"Nice work," Ethan said, breathing heavily.

"Thanks," Jax replied, giving him a thumbs-up.

From above, Tara called out. "I see the key! It's near the river!"

The group regrouped and headed toward the river. Along the way, they faced more challenges—falling rocks, deep pits, and more shadowy creatures. But each time, they worked together, combining their strengths to overcome the obstacles.

Trust and Frustrations

By the time they reached the river, everyone was tired and frustrated. Tara and Nina were arguing about the best way to cross the river, while Ethan tried to come up with a plan.

"Why don't we just use the log over there?" Jax suggested.

"That log looks too weak," Nina argued.

"We don't have time to argue!" Ethan snapped. "Let's just try it and see."

The group carefully crossed the river using the log. It wobbled dangerously, but they made it to the other side safely. Tara spotted the golden key shining in the sunlight.

"We did it!" she said, picking up the key.

Before they could celebrate, Oakheart's voice echoed again. "Well done. But remember, this was only a test. The real challenges will be much harder."

Reflections

The simulation ended, and the group found themselves back in the warehouse. They sat in a circle, catching their breath and reflecting on what had just happened.

"I think we did pretty well," Jax said, stretching his arms.

Tara shook her head. "We wasted too much time arguing. If this had been real, we might not have made it."

Nina nodded. "She's right. We need to trust each other more."

Ethan looked around at his teammates. "We'll get better. This was our first time working together. But we have to promise to listen to each other and stay focused."

The others nodded in agreement.

A Warning

Before they left, Oakheart gathered them together. His face was serious. "You made progress today, but there is still much to learn. Ravok is not just strong—he is clever. He will try to divide you and make you doubt each other. Do not let him succeed."

Ethan frowned. "Why does Ravok want to destroy the Tree of Life?"

Oakheart's eyes darkened. "Because the tree is the source of all light and life. Without it, the world will fall into darkness, and Ravok will rule over the chaos. He has tried to destroy the tree before, but now, with your help, we can stop him for good."

The group left the warehouse feeling a mix of determination and fear. They knew the road ahead would be difficult, but they were ready to face it—together.

V

The Powers Grow Stronger

The morning light streamed through the windows of the warehouse as Ethan, Jax, Tara, and Nina gathered again for another day of training. The events of the previous day had left them both excited and nervous. They had begun to uncover their powers, but they all knew they had a long way to go.

Ethan adjusted his glasses and looked around at his teammates. "So, what do you think Oakheart has planned for us today?"

"Probably more challenges," Jax said, cracking his knuckles. "I hope we get to fight something again. That bear-like thing yesterday was fun."

"Fun?" Tara said, raising an eyebrow. "It almost crushed us!"

"I agree with Tara," Nina added. "We barely made it through. We need to focus more, or we'll never be ready to face Ravok."

Before they could argue further, Oakheart appeared out of the shadows, his long cloak flowing behind him. "Good. You are all here," he said, his deep voice commanding their attention. "Today's training will push you harder. Your powers are still new, and you must learn to control them."

Understanding Each Other

Oakheart led them to a small clearing outside the warehouse. The fresh air and open space were a welcome change from the dark, confined room they had trained in the day before. In the middle of the clearing, Oakheart gestured for them to sit down in a circle.

"Before we begin, I want you to talk to each other," he said.

"Talk?" Ethan asked, confused.

"Yes. You cannot work as a team if you do not understand one another," Oakheart explained. "Tell each other about your strengths, your fears, and what drives you."

There was a moment of silence as the group exchanged uncertain glances. Finally, Ethan spoke up. "I guess I'll start. I've always been good with technology. It's just how my brain works. But... I'm not very good with people. I'm used to solving problems on my own, and I'm worried that I'll let you all down if I can't figure something out."

Tara nodded. "I understand that. I've always been creative—I love designing and making things. But sometimes, I get so focused on my ideas that I forget to listen to others. I need to work on that."

Jax smiled. "Well, I'm pretty straight forward. I've always loved sports and staying active. I guess my strength has always been physical, but I know I can be stubborn sometimes. I'm not great at waiting or following plans."

Nina hesitated before speaking. "I've always felt... different. I've never really fit in anywhere. But now, with these powers, I feel like I might have a purpose. I just don't want to mess it up."

Oakheart listened carefully as each of them spoke. When they were finished, he nodded. "Good. You are starting to understand each other. That is the first step. Now, let us move on to today's training."

Strengthening Their Powers

Oakheart led them to another part of the clearing, where several strange objects were arranged on the ground. There was a glowing sphere, a pile of bricks, a blank notebook, and a pool of water.

"These will help you practice your powers," Oakheart explained. "Ethan, you will work with the sphere. Tara, the notebook is yours. Jax, you will use the bricks. And Nina, the water will help you understand your abilities."

Ethan approached the glowing sphere cautiously. As soon as he touched it, he felt a surge of energy. Numbers, symbols, and patterns flooded his mind. He closed his eyes, focusing on the information. Slowly, the sphere began to change shape, transforming into a small robot. Ethan opened his eyes and smiled.

"Whoa, did you just make that?" Jax asked, impressed.

"I think so," Ethan said, still amazed.

Meanwhile, Tara sat down with the notebook. She picked up a pencil and began sketching. Her hand moved quickly, creating a detailed drawing of a shield. As soon as she finished, the shield appeared in front of her, solid and real.

"This is incredible," Tara said, holding the shield.

Jax, on the other hand, was busy lifting and arranging the bricks. At first, it seemed like a simple task, but as the pile grew larger, the bricks became heavier. Jax pushed himself harder, testing the limits of his strength.

"I could do this all day," he said, grinning.

Nina stood by the pool of water, unsure of what to do. She stared at her reflection, trying to focus. Slowly, her form began to shift. First, her hair turned into feathers, then her arms transformed into wings. Within moments, she had become a bird.

"I did it!" Nina said, her voice slightly different in her bird form.

The others clapped and cheered for her.

The Team Challenge

After practicing their individual powers, Oakheart called them back together. "Now, it is time for another team challenge," he said.

The clearing around them changed suddenly, just like the simulation from the day before. This time, they found themselves in a dark cave. The air was damp and cold, and the only light came from the glowing walls.

"Your task is to find the crystal hidden in this cave," Oakheart's voice echoed. "But beware—there are traps and illusions that will test your unity."

The group moved cautiously through the cave. Tara used her shield to block falling rocks, while Jax used his strength to clear debris from their path. Ethan scanned the walls for clues, and Nina transformed into a small animal to explore tight spaces.

At one point, they reached a fork in the path. One tunnel glowed faintly, while the other was completely dark.

"Which way should we go?" Tara asked.

Ethan studied the glowing path carefully. "The light looks artificial. It might be a trap. Let's try the dark tunnel."

The group agreed and moved forward. The tunnel was narrow and seemed endless, but eventually, they reached a large chamber. In the center of the room was a floating crystal, glowing with a soft blue light.

"There it is!" Jax said, running toward it.

"Wait!" Ethan shouted.

Too late. As Jax touched the crystal, the ground beneath them began to shake. The walls started closing in, and sharp spikes appeared from the ceiling.

"What do we do now?" Nina shouted.

"Work together!" Oakheart's voice echoed in their minds.

Ethan quickly analyzed the situation. "Tara, use your shield to block the spikes! Jax, hold the walls back! Nina, fly up and see if there's a way to stop this!"

Tara held her shield above them, protecting the group from the falling spikes. Jax used all his strength to push against the walls, slowing them down. Nina transformed into a bird and flew to the ceiling.

"There's a lever up here!" she called out.

"Pull it!" Ethan shouted.

Nina shifted into her human form and pulled the lever. The walls stopped moving, and the spikes retracted. The group collapsed to the ground, breathing heavily.

"That was close," Jax said, wiping sweat from his forehead.

Ethan picked up the crystal. "We did it. Together."

Lessons Learned

The simulation ended, and they were back in the clearing. Oakheart stood before them, his expression serious.

"You have made progress," he said. "But remember, this was only a test. The real danger is far greater."

The group nodded, understanding the weight of his words.

Tara looked at her teammates and smiled. "I think we're getting better at this. We just need to keep trusting each other."

"Agreed," Nina said. "We're stronger together."

Jax grinned. "And we've got some pretty awesome powers."

Ethan adjusted his glasses and looked at Oakheart. "What's next?"

Oakheart's eyes glimmered with a mix of pride and urgency. "Next, we prepare for the true battle. But first, you must rest. You will need all your strength for what lies ahead."

The group left the clearing, feeling a mix of exhaustion and determination. They knew their journey was just beginning, but they were ready to face whatever challenges came their way.

VI

Secrets of the Tree

The night was quiet, and the stars sparkled in the sky like tiny diamonds. The group sat around a small fire near the warehouse, eating the simple meal Oakheart had provided. The day's training had left them tired, but their spirits were high. They felt closer than ever as a team.

Nina poked at the fire with a stick. "Do you think Oakheart will ever tell us everything about this Tree of Life?" she asked, her voice thoughtful.

Tara shrugged. "He's keeping a lot of secrets, that's for sure. But I think he's trying to protect us."

"I don't like secrets," Jax said, his tone serious. "If we're supposed to protect the Tree, we need to know everything about it. What if we're not ready when Ravok attacks?"

Ethan adjusted his glasses. "I've been thinking the same thing. There's so much we don't know—about the Tree, about Ravok, and even about our own powers. We can't fight blindly."

Before they could discuss further, a shadow moved near the edge of the clearing. They all turned quickly, their bodies tense.

"It's just me," Oakheart said, stepping into the light. He carried a small, glowing orb in his hand. "You are asking questions. That is good. But some answers must wait."

Jax frowned. "Why? Don't you trust us?"

Oakheart sighed and sat down on a rock near the fire. "It is not about trust, Jax. It is about timing. Knowledge can be a burden, especially when you are not ready to carry it."

"But we're ready," Tara said. "We've been training hard. We've proven ourselves."

Oakheart looked at them carefully, his dark eyes unreadable. After a long pause, he nodded. "Very well. I will tell you more. But remember, what I share tonight must not leave this circle."

The group nodded eagerly, leaning closer to hear his words.

The Story of the Tree

Oakheart began to speak, his voice low and steady. "Long ago, before your world was as it is now, there was only light and darkness. The light gave life to everything—it created the stars, the oceans, and the forests. But the darkness wanted to destroy it all."

"The Tree of Life was born from this light," he continued. "Its roots stretch deep into the earth, and its branches reach high into the heavens. It is the source of all life and energy in this world. Without it, everything would fade away into nothingness."

The group listened in silence, their eyes wide with wonder.

"But the darkness did not give up," Oakheart said, his tone growing darker. "It created Ravok, a being of pure evil, to destroy the Tree. Ravok has tried many times to harm it, but he has always been stopped. Now, he is stronger than ever, and he will not stop until the Tree is gone."

"Why does he want to destroy it?" Ethan asked.

"Because without the Tree, there is no light," Oakheart explained. "And without light, the darkness can take over everything."

The Stone Beneath the Tree

"There is one more thing you must know," Oakheart said. "Beneath the Tree lies a powerful stone. This stone holds the essence of the Tree's light. If Ravok gets it, he will have the power to destroy the Tree completely. But if you use it wisely, it can stop him."

Jax sat up straighter. "Then we need to get that stone right now!"

"It is not that simple," Oakheart said. "The stone is protected by powerful magic. Only those who are truly worthy can reach it. And even then, it is not easy to use its power."

"How do we prove we're worthy?" Tara asked.

"You are already on the path," Oakheart said. "Your training, your teamwork, and your courage will show whether you are ready. But the journey to the stone will not be easy. You will face many challenges, both physical and emotional."

Nina's voice was quiet. "What happens if we fail?"

Oakheart's expression turned grave. "If you fail, the Tree will fall. And with it, your world."

A Mysterious Vision

As Oakheart spoke, the glowing orb in his hand began to pulse. The group watched in awe as the light grew brighter, casting strange shadows on the ground.

"What is that?" Ethan asked, his voice filled with curiosity.

"It is a piece of the Tree's energy," Oakheart said. "It allows me to see visions of what is to come. Would you like to see?"

The group hesitated for a moment, then nodded. Oakheart held the orb out to them, and one by one, they placed their hands on it.

The world around them seemed to fade away, replaced by a swirling vortex of colors. Images flashed before their eyes—a great battle, a dark fortress, and the Tree of Life glowing brightly against a backdrop of darkness.

They saw themselves standing together, their powers fully developed, facing a shadowy figure with glowing red eyes. The figure raised its hand, and the vision ended abruptly.

"What was that?" Nina asked, her voice shaky.

"A glimpse of the future," Oakheart said. "But the future is not set in stone. It will depend on the choices you make."

Strength in Unity

The vision left the group feeling both inspired and uneasy. They knew the path ahead would be dangerous, but they also felt a renewed sense of purpose.

"We can do this," Jax said firmly. "We just need to stick together."

Tara nodded. "We've come this far. We can't give up now."

Ethan adjusted his glasses. "If we combine our strengths, there's nothing we can't handle."

Nina smiled. "And we have Oakheart to guide us."

Oakheart's expression softened. "You have grown much since we first met. But remember, your greatest strength is not your powers. It is your unity. As long as you stand together, you will not fail."

A Shadow Looms

As the night wore on, the group fell asleep one by one, their minds filled with thoughts of the Tree and the challenges ahead. Only Oakheart remained awake, his eyes scanning the darkness.

He could feel it—a shadow moving closer, watching them from afar. Ravok's influence was growing, and time was running out.

Oakheart clenched his fists. "They are strong, but are they strong enough?" he whispered to himself.

He knew the battle for the Tree of Life was just beginning.

VII

Discovering Powers

The morning sun rose over the camp, painting the sky in shades of orange and pink. Ethan, Tara, Jax, and Nina woke up to the chirping of birds and the smell of fresh morning dew. They had spent the night thinking about the vision Oakheart had shown them. The future looked terrifying, but it also gave them a clear goal—to protect the Tree of Life at all costs.

Ethan rubbed his eyes as he sat up. "Do you think Oakheart will start training us again today?" he asked, his voice groggy.

"Probably," Tara replied, stretching her arms. "We need to be ready for anything. Ravok won't wait for us to get stronger."

Nina looked around, her sharp eyes scanning the area. "Where is Oakheart? He's usually the first one awake."

Jax shrugged. "Maybe he's off preparing something. He likes his secrets, remember?"

Before they could continue, Oakheart appeared from behind the trees, carrying a wooden staff. His expression was serious. "Good morning, my young warriors," he said.

"Today is an important day. You will begin to unlock the full potential of your powers."

The group exchanged excited but nervous glances.

The Start of Training

Oakheart led them to a clearing deeper in the forest. The area was surrounded by tall trees, their leaves forming a canopy overhead. In the center of the clearing stood a large stone circle, its surface engraved with glowing runes.

"This is the Circle of Awakening," Oakheart explained. "It will help you connect with your inner selves and discover the true extent of your abilities."

Ethan stepped forward, his curiosity piqued. "How does it work?"

Oakheart smiled faintly. "You must step into the circle one by one. The magic within it will test your mind, body, and spirit. Only by facing your fears and doubts can you unlock your powers fully."

Tara looked at the circle with a mix of excitement and hesitation. "So, who goes first?"

Jax grinned and cracked his knuckles. "I'll go. Let's see what this circle can do."

Jax's Trial

Jax stepped into the circle, and the runes began to glow brighter. A soft hum filled the air, and the ground beneath his feet seemed to vibrate. Suddenly, the world around him changed.

He found himself standing in the middle of a dark battlefield. The sky was covered in storm clouds, and the sound of clashing swords echoed in the distance. In his hand, he held a shining silver sword.

"Jax," a deep voice boomed, making him spin around. A large shadowy figure appeared before him, holding a massive axe. "You think you are strong, but strength alone will not save you."

Jax tightened his grip on the sword. "Who are you?"

"I am your doubt," the figure said. "If you cannot defeat me, you will never be worthy of your power."

The figure lunged at Jax, swinging the axe with incredible force. Jax dodged just in time and countered with his sword. The two clashed, their weapons sparking with energy.

As the battle continued, Jax realized that brute strength wasn't enough. He needed to outthink his opponent. He focused on the figure's movements, looking for weaknesses. When the figure raised its axe for another strike, Jax quickly dodged and delivered a powerful blow to its side.

The figure shattered like glass, and the battlefield disappeared. Jax was back in the clearing, his body glowing faintly.

Oakheart nodded approvingly. "Well done, Jax. You have proven your strength and your mind. Your power as the Knight of Strength is now fully awakened."

Tara's Trial

Tara was next. She stepped into the circle, her heart pounding with anticipation. As the runes glowed, the world around her shifted. She found herself in an empty room, its walls covered in blank canvases.

A voice echoed through the room. "Tara, you are a creator. But creation requires courage. Can you bring life to this empty world?"

Tara looked around, feeling overwhelmed. She had no tools, no paints—only her hands.

She closed her eyes and took a deep breath. "I can do this," she whispered to herself.

When she opened her eyes, she imagined a brush in her hand. To her surprise, a glowing paintbrush appeared. She began to draw on the canvases, her movements quick and confident.

With each stroke, the room transformed. Trees grew from the floor, birds flew through the air, and sunlight streamed through a painted window. The empty room became a vibrant forest, full of life and color.

The voice returned. "You have shown that you can create even in the face of doubt. Your power as the Wizard of Creation is now yours."

Tara smiled as the vision faded, and she returned to the clearing, her hands still glowing with magical energy.

Nina's Trial

Nina hesitated before stepping into the circle. She had always been confident, but something about this trial made her nervous.

When the world changed, she found herself in a dense forest at night. The only light came from the moon above. She heard a growl behind her and turned to see a large wolf with glowing red eyes.

The wolf lunged at her, but before it could reach her, she instinctively shapeshifted into a bird and flew into the air.

The wolf disappeared, replaced by a flock of crows that circled her menacingly. Nina shifted again, this time into a panther, and leapt to the ground.

Each time she transformed, the challenges became harder. Finally, she stood face-to-face with a mirror. In the reflection, she saw herself, but her eyes were filled with fear.

The reflection spoke. "Your true power lies in accepting who you are. Only then can you master your abilities."

Nina took a deep breath and reached out to touch the mirror. As she did, it shattered, and she felt a surge of energy.

Back in the clearing, Oakheart smiled at her. "You have embraced your true self, Nina. Your power as the Shapeshifter of Shadows is now complete."

Ethan's Trial

Ethan was the last to enter the circle. The world around him transformed into a giant laboratory filled with complex machines and glowing screens.

A robotic voice echoed in the room. "Ethan, you are the mind of the group. But intelligence without heart is meaningless. Can you solve the puzzle before you?"

Ethan looked around and saw a massive machine with gears and levers. On a screen, a timer counted down. He quickly began examining the machine, his sharp mind analyzing every detail.

As he worked, the voice spoke again. "You are running out of time. Are you sure you can do this alone?"

Ethan paused and thought about his friends. "No," he said aloud. "I can't do this alone. I need help."

The image of his friends appeared before him, each offering advice and support. With their guidance, Ethan adjusted the machine and stopped the timer just in time.

The laboratory faded, and Ethan returned to the clearing, his body glowing with a faint metallic sheen.

Oakheart placed a hand on his shoulder. "You have shown that true intelligence comes from working with others. Your power as the Technomancer is now fully awakened."

A New Beginning

With their powers fully awakened, the group felt stronger and more united than ever. They stood together in the clearing, their bodies glowing with the energy of the Tree.

Oakheart looked at them with pride. "You have all passed the trials. But this is only the beginning. The journey ahead will be filled with danger, but I believe in each of you. Together, you can protect the Tree of Life."

The group nodded, their hearts filled with determination. They knew the road ahead would be difficult, but they were ready to face it together.

VIII
The Path of Unity

The warm sunlight filtered through the forest canopy, casting golden beams on the soft ground. Ethan, Tara, Jax, Nina, and Oakheart stood in the clearing, still glowing from the energy they had gained during their trials. Each of them now had full control of their powers, but they knew their journey was far from over.

Oakheart leaned on his staff and looked at them with a serious expression. "You have passed the first test, but there is more you need to learn. Ravok is growing stronger, and his army is preparing for war. You must train harder and become a team."

Nina tilted her head, her sharp elf ears twitching slightly. "A team? We just got our powers. How are we supposed to work together so soon?"

Ethan adjusted his glasses and crossed his arms. "Nina's right. It's one thing to fight alone, but coordinating as a group is... complicated."

Oakheart smiled faintly. "That is exactly why we must start today. Follow me."

The Training Grounds

Oakheart led them to a new part of the forest. The trees here were taller, their trunks covered in glowing moss. In the middle of the clearing was a large wooden structure with ropes, ladders, and swinging platforms. A shallow stream ran alongside it, reflecting the sunlight.

"This," Oakheart said, gesturing to the structure, "is the Obstacle of Unity. It will test your teamwork and trust in each other. To succeed, you must rely on your strengths and cover each other's weaknesses."

Jax grinned, cracking his knuckles. "This looks fun. I'm ready!"

Tara gave him a playful nudge. "Don't be too confident, Jax. We're all in this together."

Ethan stepped forward, examining the structure closely. "What's the goal?"

Oakheart pointed to a glowing crystal orb at the top of the structure. "Your goal is to retrieve the orb. But be warned—this obstacle is alive. It will adapt to your strategies, and if you fail to work together, it will push you back."

The group exchanged uncertain glances.

"Let's do it," Nina said firmly, her voice filled with determination.

The Challenge Begins

The group started climbing the structure, with Jax leading the way. His super strength allowed him to lift heavy ropes and clear paths for the others. Ethan stayed at the back, analyzing the structure and suggesting strategies.

"Jax, pull that rope to the left," Ethan called out. "It should lower the ladder for Tara and Nina."

Jax did as instructed, and the ladder dropped with a loud creak. Tara quickly climbed up, using her wizarding powers to stabilize the shaking platforms with glowing magical lines.

"This is harder than it looks," Tara muttered, her hands glowing as she focused on keeping the platforms steady.

Meanwhile, Nina transformed into a hawk, soaring above the structure to scout for traps. "There's a swinging log ahead!" she shouted. "Be careful, it's moving fast."

As they moved higher, the structure began to shift. Platforms swung wildly, ropes snapped, and the ground below seemed to rise and fall like waves.

"Ethan!" Tara shouted. "We need a new plan. The structure's changing!"

Ethan's mind raced as he analyzed the shifting movements. "Tara, create a bridge with your magic! Jax, hold the bridge steady while Nina flies ahead to secure the orb!"

Tara waved her hands, and a glowing bridge of light appeared. Jax held it firmly in place, his muscles straining as the structure shook violently. Nina flew ahead, dodging swinging obstacles, and reached the orb.

"I've got it!" Nina shouted, grabbing the crystal orb with her clawed hands.

But the moment she touched the orb, the entire structure began to collapse.

A Leap of Faith

"Jump!" Oakheart shouted from below.

Nina transformed back into her human form, clutching the orb tightly as she leapt toward the ground. Tara dissolved her bridge and conjured a soft cushion of glowing leaves to break Nina's fall.

Jax grabbed Ethan and Tara, holding them close as he jumped from the collapsing structure. His super strength allowed him to land safely, though the impact sent a cloud of dust into the air.

When the dust settled, the group was on the ground, panting and covered in dirt. Nina held up the orb triumphantly. "We did it!"

Oakheart approached them, his face calm but proud. "You succeeded because you trusted each other. That is the key to defeating Ravok. Remember this lesson."

A Warning from the Shadows

As the group rested, a sudden chill filled the air. The sunlight dimmed, and the forest grew eerily quiet.

"What's happening?" Tara asked, her voice trembling.

Oakheart's expression darkened. "It's him. Ravok's presence is near."

A dark figure appeared at the edge of the clearing, its form cloaked in shadows. It didn't step closer but spoke in a deep, menacing voice.

"You think your little training will stop me?" the figure sneered. "The Tree of Life is mine, and no one can save it from me."

Jax stepped forward, his fists clenched. "Show yourself, coward!"

The figure laughed, its voice echoing through the forest. "Soon, little knight. Enjoy your victories while you can. They won't last."

With that, the figure vanished, and the forest returned to normal.

Preparing for the Fight

The group sat in a circle around a small campfire that evening, their expressions serious.

"Did you see how powerful Ravok's aura was?" Nina asked. "If that was just his shadow, imagine facing him in person."

Ethan adjusted his glasses, deep in thought. "We need more information about him. Oakheart, what do you know about Ravok's powers?"

Oakheart sighed, his eyes reflecting the flickering firelight. "Ravok was once a protector of the Tree, himself. But his greed for power consumed him. He betrayed us and tried to take the Tree's energy for himself. Now, his powers are fueled by darkness and chaos."

Tara frowned. "Is there any way to stop him for good?"

Oakheart hesitated before answering. "The only way to defeat Ravok is to strike his heart with the heartstone. But the stone is hidden beneath the Tree of Life, guarded by ancient elves who will not give it up easily."

Jax leaned forward, his face determined. "Then we'll get the stone. Whatever it takes."

A Bond of Friendship

Later that night, as the others slept, Ethan sat alone, staring at the stars. Jax walked over and sat beside him.

"Can't sleep?" he asked

Ethan shook his head. "I keep thinking about what Ravok said. What if we're not ready? What if we fail?"

Jax placed a comforting hand on his shoulder. "We won't fail, Ethan. We have each other. And Oakheart believes in us. That's enough for me."

Ethan smiled faintly. "Thanks, Jax. I needed to hear that."

In another part of the camp, Tara and Nina were talking near the fire.

"You were amazing today," Nina said, her voice sincere. "I couldn't have grabbed the orb without your creativity."

Tara grinned. "And you were incredible, flying around like that. We make a good team."

Nina smiled back. "Yeah, we do."

A New Challenge

The next morning, Oakheart gathered the group once again.

"Your training is far from over," he said. "Today, we begin the next phase. You must learn to face not only physical challenges but also the darkness within yourselves."

Ethan, Tara, Jax, and Nina exchanged uneasy glances but nodded.

"We're ready," Ethan said firmly.

Oakheart smiled. "Good. Let's begin."

IX

Ethan's Transformation

The campfire crackled softly under the starry night as the group sat together, each lost in their thoughts. After days of training and challenges, they had grown closer as a team, but the weight of their mission still loomed over them.

Oakheart stood, his staff glowing faintly in the dark. "Tomorrow, we begin a new journey. But tonight, rest well. The road ahead will test your strength and courage like never before."

The group nodded, but Ethan felt restless. He stared at the flickering flames, his mind racing.

Ethan's Restless Night

Later that night, Ethan couldn't sleep. His body felt strange, as if it didn't belong to him anymore. His hands trembled, and when he looked at them, he noticed a faint metallic sheen on his skin.

"What's happening to me?" Ethan whispered, panic rising in his chest.

He quietly left the camp and walked into the forest, hoping the cool air would calm him. But the further he walked, the worse he felt. His breathing grew shallow, and his vision flickered, like static on a screen.

Suddenly, his legs gave out, and he collapsed onto the forest floor. His body began to change—his skin turned into gleaming metal, his fingers transformed into robotic joints, and his heartbeat slowed to a mechanical hum.

"No… no!" Ethan tried to shout, but his voice came out distorted, like a robotic echo.

The Team's Discovery

The next morning, Tara woke up early and noticed that Ethan's sleeping spot was empty. She frowned and walked over to Jax and Nina, shaking them awake.

"Ethan's gone," Tara said, worry etched on her face.

Jax yawned and stretched. "Maybe he went for a walk. He does that sometimes."

Nina shook her head. "No, something feels wrong. Let's look for him."

The three of them, along with Oakheart, began searching the forest. After a short while, Tara spotted something shiny in the distance.

"Over there!" she shouted, pointing to a metallic figure slumped against a tree.

They rushed over and froze in shock. Ethan was sitting on the ground, his entire body transformed into a sleek, silver robot. His eyes glowed faintly blue, and wires pulsed under his metallic skin.

"Ethan?" Tara whispered, her voice trembling.

Ethan looked up at them, his expression filled with pain and confusion. "I… I don't know what's happening to me."

Understanding the Change

Oakheart knelt beside Ethan, examining him closely. "The transformation has begun," he said gravely.

"What transformation?" Nina asked, her voice sharp.

"Ethan is not just the smartest man in the world," Oakheart explained. "His gift is his mind, and now his body is adapting to match it. He is becoming a machine—an advanced being of technology."

Jax clenched his fists. "You knew this would happen, didn't you?"

Oakheart nodded slowly. "I suspected it. But I did not know it would happen so soon."

Ethan looked at his hands, his voice heavy with fear. "Will I stop being human?"

Oakheart placed a comforting hand on Ethan's shoulder. "Your heart and mind are still yours, Ethan. This change does not take away who you are—it makes you stronger. But you must learn to control it."

Ethan's Struggle

Over the next few days, Ethan tried to adjust to his new form. At first, he struggled to walk, his robotic legs moving stiffly. Jax helped him practice, supporting him when he stumbled.

"You'll get the hang of it," Jax said encouragingly. "Just take it one step at a time."

Tara worked with Ethan to help him understand his new abilities. She discovered that his robotic body could connect to electronic devices and analyze them instantly.

"Try connecting to this," Tara said, handing Ethan a small gadget.

Ethan focused, and a blue light flashed from his eyes. Within seconds, he had taken the gadget apart and put it back together perfectly.

"That's incredible," Tara said, smiling. "You're like a walking supercomputer."

But not everything was easy. Ethan often felt isolated, unsure if he could still relate to his friends. One evening, as they sat around the campfire, he hesitated to join their laughter.

"You're still one of us," Nina said gently, noticing his hesitation. "No matter what you look like, you're Ethan. Don't forget that."

Ethan smiled faintly. "Thanks, Nina. I needed to hear that."

The Mysterious Stranger

One evening, as the group continued their journey through the forest, they encountered a hooded figure standing on the path. The figure's face was hidden, but his presence was commanding.

"Who are you?" Jax demanded, stepping forward protectively.

The figure chuckled, his voice smooth and confident. "I'm Leo. Ravok's second-in-command."

The group tensed, readying themselves for a fight.

"Relax," Leo said, raising his hands. "I'm not here to fight you. At least, not yet."

"What do you want?" Tara asked, her eyes narrowing.

Leo smirked. "To see what you're made of. Ravok has been watching you, and he's very interested in your little group."

Nina transformed into a hawk and flew above Leo, circling him. "Why should we trust anything you say?"

"You shouldn't," Leo replied with a grin. "But let me give you some advice. If you want to stand a chance against Ravok, you'll need to be much stronger. He's preparing something big, and you're not ready."

Before anyone could respond, Leo spread his wings—massive, black, and feathered—and soared into the sky.

Doubts and Questions

After Leo disappeared, the group gathered to discuss what had happened.

"Can we believe anything he said?" Tara asked.

"I don't know," Oakheart admitted. "But one thing is clear—Ravok is watching us. We must be careful."

Jax punched a nearby tree in frustration. "I hate this! We don't even know who to trust anymore."

Nina placed a hand on his shoulder. "We trust each other. That's what matters."

Ethan, who had been quiet, finally spoke up. "Leo mentioned that Ravok is planning something big. We can't ignore that. We need to be ready."

Oakheart nodded. "Ethan is right. Your training must continue."

A New Level of Training

The next day, Oakheart introduced a new training exercise. He created an illusion of Ravok's army—a group of shadowy figures armed with swords and spears.

"These are not real," Oakheart explained. "But they will fight as if they are. You must work together to defeat them."

The group nodded and prepared for battle.

Jax charged forward, his super strength allowing him to knock down multiple enemies at once. Tara used her wizarding powers to create shields and traps, while Nina shapeshifted into a tiger, attacking with swift precision.

Ethan, now more comfortable in his robotic body, used his advanced intelligence to predict the enemies' movements.

"Tara, block the left flank!" Ethan shouted. "Jax, cover her!"

Under Ethan's guidance, the group fought with precision and coordination. By the end of the exercise, the shadowy army was defeated.

"Well done," Oakheart said, smiling. "You're becoming a true team."

A Glimpse of the Future

That night, as the group rested, Oakheart called Ethan aside.

"Ethan, your transformation is not just physical," Oakheart said. "Your mind is evolving. You can see patterns and solutions that others cannot. This will be your greatest strength."

Ethan nodded, though he still felt a twinge of doubt. "But what if I lose myself in the process? What if I stop being... me?"

Oakheart placed a hand on Ethan's shoulder. "You are more than your body, Ethan. Your heart and soul are what make you who you are. Never forget that."

Ethan took a deep breath and nodded. "I'll try."

The Journey Continues

As dawn broke, the group prepared to continue their journey. Ethan felt a renewed sense of purpose, even as he adjusted to his new form.

"We've come so far already," Tara said, looking at her friends. "But there's still so much to do."

"We'll face it together," Jax said firmly.

Nina smiled. "And we'll win."

Ethan looked at his team and felt a spark of hope. They were ready for whatever lay ahead.

As they set off, none of them knew that their greatest challenge was still to come—and that the truth about Leo would change everything.

X

The Path to Trust

The team traveled deeper into the forest, guided by Oakheart's glowing staff. Each step felt heavier as they moved closer to their next destination—a place Oakheart referred to only as "The Trials." The air was thick with tension, and although the group had grown closer, the challenges ahead made them uneasy.

Ethan, walking at the back of the group, clenched his metallic hands into fists. He had mastered his ability to switch between his human and robotic forms, but the choice weighed on him. He often wondered if his team saw him differently now that he could transform into a machine.

"I'll be fine," Ethan muttered to himself, trying to push the doubts away.

A Tense Journey

The forest was eerily quiet, except for the occasional rustle of leaves. Tara broke the silence first, glancing over her shoulder at Ethan.

"Ethan, you've been so quiet. Are you okay?" she asked.

Ethan nodded, forcing a small smile. "Yeah, just thinking."

"About what?" Nina chimed in, walking beside Tara.

"About everything," Ethan admitted. "Our mission, our powers... what comes next."

"You don't have to carry it all by yourself," Jax said firmly. He walked up and gave Ethan a friendly pat on the shoulder. "We're a team, remember?"

Ethan smiled, this time genuinely. "Thanks, Jax. I needed that."

Nina transformed into a hawk and soared above the trees. "I'll scout ahead," she called down.

"Show-off," Tara joked, grinning.

But even as they laughed, Oakheart's voice interrupted. "Stay focused. The Trials are near."

The Arrival at the Trials

They reached a clearing where the trees formed a perfect circle. In the center stood a massive stone archway covered in ancient runes. The air shimmered with energy, making the group's hair stand on end.

"This is it," Oakheart said, gesturing to the archway. "The Trials will test your trust in one another."

"Trust?" Jax repeated, raising an eyebrow.

"Yes," Oakheart confirmed. "Without trust, you cannot protect the Tree of Life. These Trials will push you to your limits. Only by working together will you succeed."

The group exchanged uneasy glances but nodded.

"We're ready," Tara said confidently.

Oakheart stepped aside, allowing them to approach the archway. One by one, they passed through, disappearing into a blinding white light.

Trial One: The Labyrinth of Fear

When the light faded, the team found themselves in a dark labyrinth. The walls were made of black stone, and an unsettling silence filled the air.

"Where are we?" Nina asked, her voice echoing.

"This must be the first trial," Ethan said, looking around.

Suddenly, the walls shifted, creating new paths and blocking others. A deep voice boomed, "Face your fears, or be lost forever."

Tara shivered. "I don't like this."

"Stay together," Jax said firmly. "No matter what happens, we don't split up."

They moved cautiously through the labyrinth, but it wasn't long before the walls began to play tricks on them. Shadows emerged, taking the shape of their worst fears.

Ethan froze as a shadowy version of himself appeared—a fully robotic figure with glowing red eyes.

"You will lose your humanity," the shadow whispered.

"No, I won't," Ethan said, stepping forward. "I control who I am, not you." He shifted into his robotic form, his blue eyes glowing brightly. With a single strike, the shadow dissolved into mist.

Nina faced a massive spider, its fangs dripping with venom. She transformed into a bear and roared, swiping at the creature until it vanished.

Tara confronted a shadow of herself, one that mocked her abilities. "You're not good enough," it sneered. But Tara drew a glowing design in the air, and the pattern came to life, obliterating the shadow.

Jax faced a collapsing ceiling, a reminder of a childhood accident that had left him trapped. He used his super strength to hold the ceiling up, his determination overpowering his fear.

One by one, they conquered their fears and found the exit to the labyrinth.

Trial Two: The River of Lies

The next trial brought them to a rushing river. The water was crystal clear, but voices echoed from it, each one planting seeds of doubt.

"Ethan doesn't trust you," the river whispered to Tara.

"Jax thinks he's better than you," it murmured to Nina.

"Tara is holding you back," it said to Ethan.

The voices grew louder, making them all hesitate.

"Don't listen to it!" Jax shouted, his voice cutting through the noise.

"But what if it's telling the truth?" Nina said quietly, her eyes darting to Ethan.

"It's not," Ethan said firmly. He stepped into the river, his robotic body unaffected by the current. He turned to the others, holding out his hand. "We trust each other, remember? That's what matters."

Tara was the first to follow, Jax and Nina joined soon after, and together they crossed the river, leaving the voices behind.

Trial Three: The Bridge of Sacrifice

The final trial led them to a narrow bridge suspended over a bottomless chasm. At the center of the bridge stood a pedestal with a glowing orb.

"To pass, one must stay behind," a voice said.

The group froze, staring at the orb.

"What does it mean, 'stay behind'?" Nina asked.

"I think it means one of us has to sacrifice ourselves," Tara said quietly.

"No way," Jax said. "We've come too far together. We're not leaving anyone behind."

Ethan stepped forward, his expression determined. "I'll do it."

"What? No!" Tara protested.

"Listen to me," Ethan said. "I can transform into a robot. If I stay behind, I might survive. You all have to finish the mission."

Jax shook his head. "We're not letting you do this."

Ethan turned to Oakheart, who had appeared at the edge of the bridge. "Is this the only way?"

Oakheart's expression was unreadable. "The choice is yours."

Ethan looked back at his friends. "Trust me. I'll be okay."

Reluctantly, the group crossed the bridge, leaving Ethan behind. As they reached the other side, the orb vanished, and Ethan reappeared beside them, unharmed.

"It was a test," Ethan said, smiling.

The Lessons Learned

As they exited the Trials, Oakheart greeted them with a proud smile.

"You have done well," he said. "You faced your fears, overcame doubt, and proved your trust in one another. You are ready for the next step."

The group exchanged tired but triumphant smiles.

"What's next?" Jax asked.

Oakheart's expression turned serious. "Now, we prepare to face Ravok."

The group nodded, ready for whatever came next. Together, they had proven that they could overcome anything.

XI

Secrets in the Shadows

The team sat around a small campfire in the middle of the forest. The stars twinkled above them, but the air felt heavy. After the Trials, they were physically and mentally exhausted. Oakheart sat nearby, sharpening the edge of his staff with a quiet focus.

Nina poked the fire with a stick. "What do you think Ravok is doing right now?" she asked, her voice quiet.

"Probably planning something evil," Jax replied, leaning back on his hands. "We'll stop him, though. We have to."

"But how?" Tara said, looking down at her hands. "The Trials were hard enough. Ravok is stronger than anything we've faced so far."

Ethan, sitting slightly apart from the group, stared into the flames. His human form was fully restored for now, but the metallic sheen of his robotic transformation still lingered in his mind. He didn't speak.

"We'll figure it out," Jax said confidently. "Together."

"Together," Nina echoed, though there was a hint of doubt in her voice.

A Sudden Disruption

Just as the mood began to lighten, a shadow moved at the edge of the campfire's light. The team froze, their eyes scanning the darkness.

"Who's there?" Jax called out, rising to his feet.

A tall figure stepped into the light. It was Leo, Ravok's sidekick. His wings glimmered faintly in the firelight, and his sharp features were unreadable.

"Leo!" Nina gasped, shifting into her bear form instinctively. "What are you doing here?"

The team jumped into defensive positions. Tara summoned a glowing staff, Jax clenched his fists, and Ethan's arm shifted into a robotic blaster.

"I come in peace," Leo said, raising his hands. His voice was calm but firm.

Oakheart stood up, his eyes narrowing. "Why would Ravok's sidekick come here in peace?"

"I'm not who you think I am," Leo said slowly. "I need to talk to you. All of you."

The team hesitated, unsure whether to trust him.

"Give me one good reason not to fight you right now," Jax said, stepping forward.

"Because I'm not Ravok's ally," Leo said. "I'm a protector of the Tree of Life—just like you."

A Shocking Revelation

Silence fell over the camp. The team exchanged stunned glances, and Oakheart's grip on his staff tightened.

"You're lying," Tara said, her voice shaking. "You've been working with Ravok this whole time!"

"I had to," Leo explained. "Ravok doesn't know my true identity. I've been working as a double agent, trying to sabotage his plans from the inside."

Ethan's robotic hand shifted back to human form as he stepped closer to Leo. "If that's true, then why are you telling us now?"

"Because time is running out," Leo said. "Ravok is planning an attack on the Tree of Life. If we don't stop him, he'll destroy it—and everything connected to it."

Oakheart studied Leo carefully. "If what you say is true, then you've been risking your life all this time."

"I have," Leo said, his wings folding behind him. "But I couldn't stand by and watch Ravok win."

Trust or Doubt

The group huddled together, whispering urgently.

"Do we trust him?" Nina asked.

"He could be lying," Tara said, crossing her arms.

"But what if he's not?" Jax argued. "If he's really on our side, we need him."

Ethan stayed quiet, thinking deeply. Finally, he spoke. "Leo, if you're telling the truth, then prove it. Tell us something only a protector of the Tree of Life would know."

Leo nodded. "The Tree isn't just a source of power. It's alive. Its roots stretch across the entire world, connecting every living thing. Underneath the Tree, there's a hidden chamber. That's where the Heartstone is kept—the only thing that can stop Ravok for good."

Oakheart's eyes widened slightly, but he quickly masked his reaction.

"Okay," Ethan said, nodding. "I believe him."

"Are you sure?" Tara asked.

"Yes," Ethan said firmly. "We don't have time to waste. If Leo's telling the truth, we need his help."

Preparing for Battle

Leo stepped closer to the fire, and the tension eased slightly. "If we're going to stop Ravok, we need to act quickly," he said.

"What's his plan?" Oakheart asked.

"He's gathering an army," Leo explained. "Dark creatures from the Shadow Realm. He plans to attack the Tree of Life in three days."

"Three days?" Nina repeated, her eyes widening. "That's not enough time!"

"It's all we have," Leo said. "But there's one advantage we can use. Ravok doesn't know that you're ready. He thinks you're still weak."

Oakheart nodded. "Then we'll use that to our advantage. We'll strike before he does."

Leo hesitated. "There's one more thing. Ravok knows about the Heartstone. He's searching for it too. If he gets it before we do, we won't stand a chance."

The team exchanged worried glances.

"Then we have to find it first," Ethan said, his voice steady.

A New Mission

Oakheart stood and addressed the group. "Our mission is clear. We must locate the Heartstone before Ravok. Leo, do you know where it is?"

"Yes," Leo said. "But it won't be easy to get to. The chamber beneath the Tree is protected by powerful magic—and by the Elves of the Roots."

"The Elves of the Roots?" Tara asked.

"They're ancient guardians," Oakheart explained. "They live beneath the Tree of Life, protecting its secrets. They won't let anyone pass without a fight."

"Great," Jax muttered. "Another fight."

"We can handle it," Ethan said. He looked at Leo. "You're with us now. If we work together, we can do this."

Leo nodded, a small smile forming on his face. "Thank you. I won't let you down."

Setting Out

The next morning, the team packed their supplies and prepared to leave. Leo led the way, his wings helping him navigate the dense forest. Oakheart stayed close behind, his staff glowing faintly in the early light.

As they walked, Ethan found himself walking beside Leo.

"Why didn't you tell us sooner?" Ethan asked.

"I wanted to," Leo said. "But I had to be sure you were ready. The Trials proved that you are."

Ethan nodded, though doubt still lingered in his mind. "Do you think we can really beat Ravok?"

"We have to," Leo said simply.

The Journey Beneath

After hours of walking, the group reached the base of the Tree of Life. Its massive trunk stretched high into the sky, and its roots twisted deep into the earth.

"This is it," Leo said. "The entrance to the chamber is hidden among the roots."

Oakheart stepped forward, placing his hand on the bark of the Tree. He whispered an ancient phrase, and the ground beneath them trembled.

A hidden doorway appeared at the base of the Tree, leading into darkness.

"Stay close," Oakheart said, stepping inside.

The team followed, their footsteps echoing in the narrow tunnel. The air grew cooler as they descended, and the faint sound of flowing water reached their ears.

The Guardians Appear

As they reached the chamber, they found themselves surrounded by glowing roots. The Heartstone rested on a pedestal in the center, its light pulsating softly.

But before they could take another step, figures emerged from the shadows. The Elves of the Roots had arrived.

"Who dares enter our domain?" one of them demanded, their voice echoing through the chamber.

"We mean no harm," Oakheart said, stepping forward. "We seek the Heartstone to protect the Tree of Life."

The Elves exchanged glances before drawing their weapons. "Prove your worth," their leader said.

The team braced themselves as the Elves attacked.

The Fight for the Heartstone

The chamber erupted into chaos as the team fought the Elves. Tara used her magic to create glowing barriers, blocking attacks. Jax charged forward, his super strength knocking down enemies. Nina shifted into a tiger, her claws slashing through the air.

Ethan transformed into his robotic form, his blaster firing precise shots. He felt the weight of his dual nature but focused on protecting his team.

Leo leaped into the air, using his wings to outmaneuver the Elves. His movements were quick and calculated, showing his years of training.

Despite their strength, the team struggled against the Elves' skill and magic.

The Turning Point

Ethan noticed a pattern in the Elves' movements. "They're protecting the Heartstone!" he shouted.

"Then we need to distract them," Leo said. "Ethan, can you create a diversion?"

Ethan nodded. He charged forward, drawing the Elves' attention. Meanwhile, Leo flew toward the pedestal, reaching for the Heartstone.

The leader of the Elves tried to stop him, but Oakheart intervened, using his staff to block the attack.

With one final push, Leo grabbed the Heartstone. The chamber filled with light, and the Elves froze, their weapons lowering.

"You have proven your worth," the leader said. "The golden Hearthstone is yours."

A Moment of Triumph

The team stood together, breathing heavily but victorious. The Heartstone glowed brightly in Leo's hands, its power resonating through the chamber.

"We did it," Tara said, a smile spreading across her face.

"This is just the beginning," Oakheart said. "Ravok will come for us, but now we have a chance."

Leo looked at the team, his expression serious. "Thank you for trusting me. Together, we can protect the Tree of Life."

Ethan placed a hand on Leo's shoulder. "We're in this together."

As they left the chamber, the group felt a renewed sense of purpose. The fight against Ravok was far from over, but they were ready to face whatever came next—together.

XII
Family Secrets Revealed

The journey back from the Heartstone Chamber was quieter than usual. Everyone felt the weight of what lay ahead. They had the Heartstone now, but Ravok would stop at nothing to destroy the Tree of Life.

Tara walked alongside Ethan, her thoughts swirling. She glanced at Leo, who carried the glowing Heartstone in his satchel. Something about him seemed familiar, but she couldn't quite place it. His confident stride, the way he spoke, and his sharp features all tugged at a memory she couldn't fully recall.

Leo noticed Tara watching him and gave her a small smile. "You okay?" he asked.

Tara nodded quickly. "Yeah, I'm fine."

Ethan's robotic arm shifted slightly as he adjusted his grip on his blaster. "We should pick up the pace. If Ravok's spies are tracking us, we can't let them catch up."

Oakheart led the group through the dense forest, his staff glowing faintly to light the way. "We're close to the camp," he said. "We'll rest there and plan our next move."

A Stormy Night

By the time they reached the camp, dark clouds had gathered overhead. The air was heavy, and a light drizzle began to fall. Oakheart lit a small fire, and the group huddled around it for warmth.

Jax stretched his arms, looking exhausted but determined. "So, what's the plan now? We've got the Heartstone, but how do we use it to stop Ravok?"

"The Heartstone must be placed directly into Ravok's heart," Oakheart explained. "It's the only way to trap him and protect the Tree."

"That sounds... impossible," Nina said, shifting nervously in her seat. "How are we supposed to get close enough to do that?"

"We'll find a way," Ethan said firmly. His determination was unshaken, but the others could see the tension in his robotic fingers.

Leo remained quiet, staring into the fire. Tara noticed his unusual silence and decided to speak to him.

"Leo," she said softly, "you've been quiet ever since we left the chamber. Is something wrong?"

Leo looked up, his expression conflicted. "There's something I need to tell you," he said.

The rest of the group turned to look at him, curiosity and concern etched on their faces.

The Truth Comes Out

Leo hesitated, his wings twitching slightly. "Tara... I didn't come here just to help you fight Ravok. There's something more."

"What do you mean?" Tara asked, frowning.

Leo took a deep breath. "I'm your brother."

The words hung in the air, and the group froze. Tara stared at him, her mind racing. "What? That's not possible."

"It is," Leo said, his voice steady. "My full name is Leo Frost. I'm your older brother."

Tara shook her head, disbelief and confusion clouding her thoughts. "No... I don't have a brother. My family—"

"Your family is more than you know," Leo interrupted gently. "Our father was one of the original protectors of the Tree of Life. He dedicated his life to guarding its power."

Tara's eyes widened. Memories of her father, long buried, began to resurface. He had always been kind and protective, but he had kept many secrets. "Why didn't I know this?"

"Our father wanted to keep you safe," Leo explained. "He knew that being a protector came with dangers. He thought the best way to protect you was to keep you away from the Tree—and from me."

Tara's voice trembled. "Why are you telling me this now?"

"Because you deserve to know the truth," Leo said. "And because our father's sacrifice is the reason we're here today."

Memories of the Past

Leo reached into his satchel and pulled out a small, worn notebook. He handed it to Tara. "This belonged to our father. It's his journal. It explains everything."

Tara hesitated before taking the journal. The leather cover was cracked and weathered, and the pages were filled with neat handwriting. She opened it carefully, her eyes scanning the words.

"The Tree of Life is more than just a source of power. It is the heart of our world, connecting all living things. As a protector, my duty is to guard it with my life. My children, Leo and Tara, must never know the dangers I face. I only hope they grow up safe and happy."

Tara's hands trembled as she read. Tears welled up in her eyes, but she quickly wiped them away. "Why didn't he tell me?" she whispered.

"He wanted to shield you from the danger," Leo said. "But when he died, I took up his role as a protector. I've been working to honor his legacy ever since."

A Sibling Bond

The group watched the emotional exchange in silence, unsure of what to say. Finally, Ethan spoke. "Leo, why didn't you tell us earlier?"

"I wanted to," Leo admitted. "But I wasn't sure if Tara—or any of you—would trust me. I needed to prove myself first."

Tara looked at Leo, her emotions a mix of anger, sadness, and a growing sense of connection. "I don't know if I can forgive you for keeping this from me," she said honestly. "But... I believe you."

Leo's expression softened. "That's all I could hope for."

Nina reached out and placed a comforting hand on Tara's shoulder. "You're not alone in this," she said. "We're all in this together."

Jax nodded. "Yeah. Family or not, we've got your back."

A New Resolve

As the rain continued to fall, Tara closed the journal and handed it back to Leo. "Thank you for telling me," she said quietly. "I need some time to process this, but I'm glad I know the truth."

Leo nodded, understanding. "Take all the time you need. We'll get through this—together."

Oakheart cleared his throat, drawing the group's attention. "This revelation changes nothing about our mission," he said. "If anything, it strengthens our resolve. The bond you share as siblings will only make us stronger."

Ethan stood and faced the group. "Ravok won't wait for us to sort out our feelings. We need to keep moving."

"Agreed," Oakheart said. "We'll rest tonight and continue our journey at first light."

A Quiet Moment

Later that night, as the others slept, Tara sat by the fire, deep in thought. Leo approached her cautiously, sitting down a few feet away.

"Do you remember him?" Leo asked softly.

"Our father?" Tara said. "A little. He was always busy, always traveling. I didn't understand why back then."

"He loved you," Leo said. "He talked about you all the time. He wanted to keep you safe more than anything."

Tara looked at Leo, her expression softening. "What was he like as a protector?"

Leo smiled faintly. "He was brave and wise. He believed in the power of the Tree and the importance of protecting it. He trained me when I was old enough, but he never wanted you to be involved. He thought you deserved a normal life."

Tara nodded slowly. "I wish I had known him better. But... I'm glad I have you."

Leo's smile grew. "I'm glad I have you too, little sister."

Preparing for the Fight

The next morning, the group packed up their camp and set off toward their next destination. The forest grew denser, and the path became more treacherous, but their resolve was stronger than ever.

As they walked, Oakheart spoke to the group. "Our next challenge will be to find Ravok's base. He's hidden it well, but with the Heartstone, we might be able to locate it."

"Do you think he knows we have it?" Nina asked.

"Most likely," Oakheart said. "Which means we need to be ready for anything."

Ethan glanced at Tara and Leo, who were walking side by side. "You two okay?"

Tara nodded. "Yeah. We're okay."

Leo added, "Stronger than ever."

A New Threat

As the group pressed on, the forest grew darker. The air felt heavier, and an eerie silence surrounded them.

"Something's not right," Jax said, his eyes scanning the shadows.

Suddenly, a low growl echoed through the trees. Dark creatures began to emerge from the shadows, their glowing red eyes fixed on the group.

"Shadow Beasts," Oakheart said grimly. "Ravok's minions."

The team quickly formed a defensive circle, their weapons and powers ready.

"Let's show them what we've got," Ethan said, his robotic arm transforming into a blaster.

A Fierce Battle

The Shadow Beasts attacked, their claws slashing through the air. Tara summoned glowing shields to protect the group, while Nina shifted into a lion, roaring fiercely as she charged at the creatures.

Jax used his super strength to knock the beasts back, and Ethan's precise shots took down several enemies. Leo took to the air, his wings giving him an advantage as he struck from above.

Despite their efforts, the beasts kept coming. Oakheart used his staff to create a barrier, but it wouldn't hold for long.

"We need to find their source!" Leo shouted.

Tara nodded. "Let's end this!"

As the battle raged on, the group worked together, their bond stronger than ever. They knew that this was just the beginning of the fight against Ravok, but they were ready to face whatever came next—together.

XIII

A Dangerous Journey

The group stood in the clearing, surrounded by the fallen Shadow Beasts. Their breathing was heavy, and their clothes were torn, but they were victorious. The forest had grown silent again, but the sense of danger lingered.

Ethan adjusted his robotic arm, which had shifted back to its regular form. "That was too close," he said, scanning the dark forest. "We can't keep fighting like this forever. We need a plan."

Oakheart stepped forward, his staff glowing faintly. "Ravok is testing us," he said. "These attacks are meant to weaken our resolve. But we must push forward. The Tree of Life depends on us."

Tara wiped sweat from her brow, her magical shield fading. She glanced at Leo, who stood nearby with his wings folded. His presence still felt strange to her. Knowing he was her brother changed everything, but they hadn't had time to fully talk about it.

"Where do we go now?" Nina asked, shifting back into her human form. She looked tired, but her eyes were sharp with determination.

Oakheart raised his staff, pointing toward the horizon. "There is a hidden path through the mountains. It will take us closer to Ravok's fortress. But the journey is dangerous. We'll need to move quickly."

Jax flexed his muscles and cracked his knuckles. "Dangerous or not, we don't have a choice. Let's go."

Through the Mountains

The group traveled for hours, the forest giving way to rocky terrain. The air grew colder, and the wind howled through the mountains. The narrow path was treacherous, with loose stones and steep drops on either side.

Ethan took the lead, his sharp mind analyzing the safest way forward. "Watch your step," he called back to the others. "One wrong move, and it's a long way down."

Tara followed closely, using her magic to steady herself when the ground shifted beneath her feet. Behind her, Nina transformed into a mountain goat, her agile steps making it easier to navigate the rocky path.

Leo flew above the group, keeping watch for any signs of danger. His sharp eyes scanned the horizon, but all he could see were endless peaks and valleys.

Jax, who was carrying most of the supplies, grumbled under his breath. "I'm all for saving the world, but couldn't Ravok pick a fortress that's easier to reach?"

Oakheart chuckled softly. "Evil rarely makes things easy, Jax. That's why we must be strong."

As the sun began to set, the group reached a small plateau where they decided to rest.

A Quiet Conversation

While the others set up camp, Tara approached Leo. He was sitting on a rock, looking out at the distant peaks.

"Hey," she said softly, sitting down beside him.

Leo turned to her, his expression unreadable. "Hey."

Tara hesitated before speaking. "I've been thinking about what you told me. About our father."

Leo nodded, his gaze shifting to the horizon. "I know it's a lot to take in. I didn't mean to keep it from you for so long."

"I understand why you did," Tara said. "But it still feels… strange. I always thought I knew who I was. Now it feels like there's this whole other part of me I never knew about."

Leo smiled faintly. "Our father would be proud of you, Tara. You've become stronger than I ever imagined."

Tara looked at him, her eyes filled with determination. "I want to honor his legacy. But more than that, I want to protect the people I care about. That includes you."

Leo's expression softened. "And I'll do everything I can to protect you, little sister."

The Ambush

Their quiet moment was interrupted by a sudden roar. The ground shook, and large boulders tumbled down the mountainside.

"Everyone, get ready!" Oakheart shouted, his staff glowing brightly.

From the shadows, a group of Ravok's soldiers emerged. These weren't ordinary soldiers; they were heavily armored and moved with unnatural speed.

Ethan's arm transformed into a blaster, and he fired a series of precise shots. "They found us!"

Nina shifted into a panther, her sleek form darting through the chaos as she took down two soldiers with swift, powerful strikes.

Tara summoned her magical shields, protecting Jax as he charged into the fray with his super strength. He lifted a boulder and hurled it at the enemy, sending them scattering.

Leo soared above the battlefield, using his wings to maneuver quickly. He struck from above, his attacks precise and calculated.

Despite their efforts, the soldiers kept coming and they lost the stone . Oakheart created a barrier of light, but it wouldn't hold for long.

"We need to retreat!" Ethan shouted. "There are too many of them!"

"No," Oakheart said firmly. "We must fight. If we run now, they'll follow us to the Tree of Life."

A Risky Plan

Ethan's mind raced as he analyzed the situation. His robotic enhancements allowed him to calculate probabilities and devise strategies in seconds.

"Tara!" he called out. "Can you create a distraction?"

Tara nodded, focusing her energy. She drew a glowing symbol in the air, and a burst of light erupted, blinding the soldiers.

"Now's our chance!" Ethan shouted. "Leo, Nina, cover us!"

Leo and Nina sprang into action, holding off the soldiers while the rest of the group regrouped.

"We need to split up," Ethan said. "If we stay together, they'll overwhelm us."

Oakheart hesitated but eventually nodded. "Ethan's right. Jax and I will lead one group. Tara, Nina, and Leo, you'll take the another route and head toward the fortress."

"What about you?" Tara asked.

"I'll stay with Jax," Oakheart said. "We'll create a diversion and draw the soldiers away."

Reluctantly, the group agreed. They split up, each team heading in a different direction.

Tara's Team

Tara, Nina, and Leo moved quickly through the mountains. The path was steep and dangerous, but they pushed forward, knowing the fate of the Tree of Life depended on them.

"I don't like leaving them behind," Tara said, her voice filled with worry.

"They'll be fine," Leo assured her. "Oakheart knows what he's doing."

Nina, still in her panther form, growled softly. She seemed tense, her ears twitching at every sound.

Suddenly, the ground beneath them gave way, and they tumbled into a hidden cave.

The Hidden Cave

The cave was dark and damp, with faintly glowing crystals embedded in the walls. The air was cold, and the sound of dripping water echoed around them.

"Is everyone okay?" Tara asked, brushing dirt off her clothes.

"I'm fine," Leo said, helping her to her feet.

Nina shifted back into her human form, shaking her head. "What is this place?"

Leo examined the crystals on the walls. "It looks like an ancient refuge. Maybe one of the protectors used it long ago."

As they explored the cave, they discovered a small pedestal in the center. On it lay a glowing map.

Tara picked up the map carefully. "This shows the way to Ravok's fortress," she said, her voice filled with awe.

Leo studied the map. "It also shows a secret entrance. This could be our best chance to get inside without being noticed."

"But why would this be here?" Nina asked, her brow furrowed.

"Maybe it's fate," Tara said softly.

A Growing Bond

As they prepared to leave the cave, Tara turned to Leo. "You've been a protector for a long time, haven't you?"

Leo nodded. "Ever since our father passed. It's not an easy life, but it's one I'm proud of."

Tara smiled faintly. "I think he'd be proud of you too."

Leo's expression softened. "And he'd be proud of you, Tara. You've come so far, and you're stronger than you realize."

Nina, watching the siblings, smiled to herself. Despite the danger they faced, their bond was growing stronger.

As they emerged from the cave, the sun was setting, casting the mountains in shades of orange and gold. The path ahead was still dangerous, but they felt a renewed sense of purpose.

With the map in hand and the teamwork in their possession, they knew they were one step closer to defeating Ravok and protecting the Tree of Life.

But deep in the shadows, Ravok's spies watched their every move, ready to report back to their master.

The battle was far from over.

XIV

The Hidden Fortress

The map they found in the cave led them through a maze of narrow trails, steep cliffs, and hidden valleys. Tara held the glowing map tightly, her eyes scanning it to make sure they were on the right path. The map's light pulsed faintly, as if guiding them toward their destination.

"This way," Tara said, pointing to a narrow trail that curved around the edge of a mountain.

Leo, walking slightly ahead, glanced back. "We need to be careful. If Ravok's spies are watching, this trail will be the perfect spot for an ambush."

Nina, in her hawk form, soared above them, keeping watch. She screeched once and then swooped down to land beside Tara, shifting back into her human form.

"No enemies nearby," Nina said, brushing dust from her sleeves. "But I saw movement far off in the distance. We need to hurry."

The group pressed forward, their determination outweighing their exhaustion.

The Shadow Sentinel

As they approached a rocky outcrop, the air grew colder, and the sky darkened unnaturally. The group stopped in their tracks, their eyes fixed on the figure standing in their path.

It was a Shadow Sentinel, one of Ravok's elite guardians. The Sentinel was tall and cloaked in black armor that seemed to shimmer with dark energy. Its glowing red eyes locked onto the group.

"You dare come this far?" the Sentinel's voice boomed, echoing through the mountains. "Turn back now, or face your doom."

Leo stepped forward, his wings spreading wide. "We're not afraid of you."

The Sentinel laughed, a deep, menacing sound. "Then you are fools."

Before anyone could react, the Sentinel raised its hand, and a wave of dark energy surged toward them.

A Fierce Battle

"Spread out!" Leo shouted, taking to the air to avoid the attack.

Tara quickly drew a glowing rune in the air, creating a shield that blocked the energy wave. "Nina, flank it!" she yelled.

Nina shifted into a sleek black panther and darted to the side, her movements silent and quick. She leaped at the Sentinel, claws slashing, but her attack bounced off its armor.

Ethan's voice crackled through their communication devices. "Tara, distract it! I've got an idea."

Tara nodded and summoned a burst of light, blinding the Sentinel temporarily. "Over here!" she taunted, drawing its attention.

Ethan, who had stayed behind to work on a plan, emerged from the shadows in his robotic form. His body glowed with energy as he raised his arm, now transformed into a powerful cannon.

"Everyone, get clear!" Ethan shouted.

The group dove out of the way as Ethan fired a concentrated beam of energy. The blast struck the Sentinel directly, shattering its armor and sending it crashing to the ground.

A Secret Entrance

With the Sentinel defeated, the group continued along the trail. The map's glow grew brighter, and soon they found themselves standing before a massive stone wall.

"This must be it," Tara said, examining the map. "The secret entrance to Ravok's fortress."

Leo ran his hand along the wall, feeling for hidden mechanisms. "There's got to be a way to open it."

Nina, now in her elf form, closed her eyes and placed her hands on the stone. "There's magic here," she said. "Dark magic. But I think I can undo it."

Tara stepped forward to help, her own magic blending with Nina's as they worked together to break the enchantment.

After a few tense moments, the stone wall began to shift, revealing a hidden passageway.

"We're in," Leo said, his voice low. "But we need to stay alert. Ravok won't make this easy for us."

Inside the Fortress

The passageway led them into the heart of Ravok's fortress. The air was thick with the smell of damp stone and burning torches. The walls were lined with intricate carvings depicting battles and conquests, all glorifying Ravok's dark reign.

"This place gives me the creeps," Nina whispered, her eyes scanning the shadows.

Leo nodded. "It's designed to intimidate. Don't let it get to you."

Ethan, back in his human form, studied the layout of the fortress. "According to the map, the Heartstone chamber is just ahead. But I'm guessing it's heavily guarded."

As they moved deeper into the fortress, they encountered several traps—spiked walls, collapsing floors, and hidden arrows. Ethan's sharp mind and robotic reflexes proved invaluable in detecting and disarming them.

"Ravok really doesn't want anyone getting through here," Ethan muttered as he deactivated another trap.

The Guardian's Test

When they finally reached the Heartstone chamber, they were met with an unexpected challenge. Standing in front of the chamber door was a massive golem made of obsidian and fire. Its glowing eyes fixed on the group, and it let out a deafening roar.

"This must be the final guardian," Tara said, gripping her staff tightly.

Leo spread his wings and took to the air. "We'll have to work together to take it down."

The battle was intense. The golem's fiery attacks forced the group to stay on the move, dodging and countering whenever they could.

Tara used her magic to create barriers and launch attacks from a distance. Nina shifted into a dragon, her fiery breath matching the golem's flames. Leo struck from above, using his agility to stay out of the golem's reach.

Ethan transformed back into his robotic form, his advanced weaponry giving the team a much-needed edge. "Keep it distracted!" he called out as he aimed for the golem's weak points.

After what felt like an eternity, the golem let out one final roar and crumbled into a pile of glowing embers.

The Heartstone Chamber

With the guardian defeated, the group entered the Heartstone chamber. The room was vast and circular, with walls covered in ancient runes. In the center of the room stood two pedestals, each holding a glowing crystal—one pulsating with a warm, golden light and the other radiating a darker, more intense red glow.

Tara's eyes widened as she approached the golden Heartstone. "This is it," she said, her voice filled with awe. "This is the one we've been searching for—the key to defeating Ravok."

Leo looked at the other pedestal, his eyes narrowing. "And that one?"

Tara stepped closer to the other Heartstone, the red one. "I'm not sure, but it feels powerful... dangerous."

Nina, who had been silently observing, spoke up. "The Heartstones are connected to the Tree of Life. One may hold the power to protect it, while the other could destroy everything."

Tara's hand hovered over the golden Heartstone, and she carefully lifted it from the pedestal. The moment she touched it, the crystal's energy surged, filling her with warmth.

"We have to take both," Leo said. "We can't risk leaving either one behind."

Tara nodded, carefully cradling the Heartstone in her hands. "I'll take this one," she said. "But the other..."

Leo stepped forward, his wings unfurled as he gently took the red Heartstone. "I'll keep this one safe. It may be the key to stopping Ravok and protecting the Tree of Life."

With both Heartstones now in their possession, the group turned to leave the chamber. But Tara's mind raced—what exactly was the second Heartstone's true purpose? She had no doubt that the golden one would help defeat Ravok, but the red one still felt like a mystery.

The Escape

As they made their way back through the fortress, the air began to shake. The walls groaned under pressure, and the ceiling above them cracked. "Ravok knows we're here," Leo said, his voice tight with urgency. "We need to move faster!"

Ethan, in his robotic form, scanned their surroundings. "The exits are blocked. We'll have to find another way out."

With the two Heartstones in hand, they rushed down a different corridor, dodging falling debris. Tara's hand was firmly gripping the golden Heartstone, but her mind couldn't stop thinking about the red one.

Why did it feel so different? What powers did it hold?

The Hidden Path

As the group reached a dead-end in the corridor, Tara spotted something unusual—a hidden door covered by moss and vines. She brushed her hand across the stone, revealing an old, intricate carving that glowed faintly.

"This must be the way out," Tara said, touching the Heartstone to the door's carving. The crystal's light merged with the carving's glow, and the door creaked open, revealing a hidden passage.

Leo's eyes darkened. "Let's go. We don't have much time."

As the group ventured through the passage, Tara glanced at the red Heartstone in Leo's hands. "I still don't understand why it feels so different from mine."

Leo looked down at it, his expression unreadable. "Maybe it's not meant to be understood, at least not yet. But I'll make sure it stays safe."

Nina nodded. "We have the Heartstones. Now we need to get back to Oakheart and find a way to use them together."

The passageway opened up into a large cavern, where they found an exit leading outside. The group quickly climbed up the rocky terrain and emerged into the open air.

The Return to Oakheart

The journey back to Oakheart's sanctuary was tense. With the Heartstones in their possession, they knew Ravok would soon be coming for them. The team needed to rest, plan, and prepare for the final battle.

When they arrived, Oakheart was waiting for them. His wise eyes scanned the Heartstones, and he gave a solemn nod.

"You've done well," Oakheart said, his voice deep. "But the true test has yet to come. Ravok is preparing for his next move, and with both Heartstones, you'll have the power to stop him. But remember, they must be used in unison."

Tara looked at the two Heartstones, feeling the weight of their responsibility. "What exactly will happen when we use them together?"

Oakheart's gaze softened. "The golden Heartstone holds the power of life—the power to protect. The red Heartstone, however, holds the power of destruction. If used incorrectly, it could tear everything apart."

Leo's voice was serious. "We'll make sure to use them the right way."

XV

The Heartstone's Power

The sun was beginning to set as the group stood in Oakheart's sanctuary, their minds filled with worry. Tara and Leo each held a Heartstone—one glowing with a golden light, the other pulsating with a dangerous red energy. They had returned to Oakheart after narrowly escaping Ravok's fortress, and now, the weight of the task ahead seemed even heavier than before.

Oakheart stood in front of them, his expression serious and thoughtful. "You've done well to retrieve the Heartstones," he said, his voice deep and calm. "But we are not yet ready for the final battle. The Heartstones are more powerful than you can imagine. We must understand them fully before we attempt to use them."

Tara held the golden Heartstone tightly in her hand, feeling its warmth. It pulsed with a soft glow, as if responding to her touch. She glanced at the red Heartstone in Leo's hands, its energy dark and intense. There was no doubt that these two objects held unimaginable power, but Tara couldn't shake the feeling that they were not meant to be wielded carelessly.

"What do we do now?" Jax asked, his eyes scanning the room, restless.

Oakheart turned to face him. "We must learn the true nature of the Heartstones and prepare yourselves for the journey ahead. There is a way to unlock their full power, but it requires time, patience, and understanding."

Tara stepped forward, her heart racing. "Oakheart, how can we use them together? How do we stop Ravok?"

The ancient protector's eyes softened. "The two Heartstones are connected to the Tree of Life itself. One represents creation—the golden Heartstone—and the other represents destruction—the red Heartstone. Only when used together, in perfect harmony, can they stop Ravok."

"But how do we control the red one?" Leo asked, his voice filled with concern. "Its power feels dangerous. I can feel its pull, and I don't want to risk using it incorrectly."

Oakheart nodded gravely. "The red Heartstone is a dangerous weapon. It is meant to destroy, to bring an end to evil. But it can also bring destruction to everything around it if misused. That is why the golden Heartstone is equally important. It can balance the power of the red Heartstone, bringing life where destruction might take place."

Tara held the golden Heartstone tightly in her hand, feeling its warmth and energy. "I'll be careful with it," she said, her voice determined. "We can't let Ravok win. We need to end this."

Oakheart gave her a long, steady look. "You are ready, but the task will not be easy. Ravok is stronger than ever, and his army grows every day. He will stop at nothing to claim the Heartstones for himself. You must remain vigilant and work together. Only then can you succeed."

The team stood in silence for a moment, contemplating Oakheart's words. The path ahead was unclear, but one thing was certain—the final battle was approaching, and the Heartstones were their only hope.

Preparing for Battle

The next few days were spent training and preparing. Oakheart guided them through exercises that helped unlock the potential of the Heartstones. Tara practiced controlling the golden Heartstone's energy, learning how to use its power to create shields, heal wounds, and protect the group. Leo focused on learning how to wield the red Heartstone, understanding its destructive force and how to use it in tandem with the golden Heartstone.

Ethan, in his robotic form, worked tirelessly with the team, using his advanced intelligence to analyze Ravok's army and plan their attack. Jax and Nina trained together, strengthening their skills and abilities. Every day, they grew stronger, more connected, and more determined.

But despite their progress, a sense of unease lingered. They knew that Ravok was not far behind, and that the time to confront him was rapidly approaching.

One evening, as the group sat around a fire in the sanctuary, Tara looked up at Oakheart. "Are we ready?" she asked quietly.

Oakheart looked at her with a calm expression. "No one can ever be fully ready for such a battle. But you have trained, you have bonded, and you have proven that you can work together. Now, you must trust in yourselves and each other."

Tara nodded, her fingers still holding the golden Heartstone. She felt its warmth and its promise of hope. She could feel the energy of the Tree of Life flowing through it, connecting her to something much larger than herself.

"We'll do it," Leo said firmly, holding the red Heartstone tightly. "We'll stop Ravok, no matter what."

The Final Journey

The next morning, the group set out for Ravok's fortress. The journey was long and treacherous, but they pressed on, their determination unshaken. As they neared Ravok's stronghold, the air grew heavier, charged with dark energy. The Heartstones pulsed in their hands, responding to the presence of their enemy.

Ravok's fortress loomed ahead, dark and imposing. The team stood at the entrance, ready to face whatever awaited them inside. Tara felt her heart race, but she knew that there was no turning back. This was the moment they had been preparing for.

"Stay close," Leo instructed, his voice steady. "We'll make it through this, together."

With the two Heartstones in hand, they entered the fortress, their footsteps echoing through the dark halls. The walls were lined with ominous runes, and the air felt thick with the power of Ravok's dark magic. Tara could feel the energy of the Heartstones growing stronger, as if they were guiding her toward the final confrontation.

As they ventured deeper into the fortress, they encountered Ravok's forces. Creatures twisted by dark magic, each more powerful than the last, attacked them from every direction. But the team fought with everything they had, using their combined powers to push forward.

Tara summoned the power of the golden Heartstone, creating barriers of light to protect them. Leo unleashed the destructive force of the red Heartstone, striking down enemies with powerful blasts. Ethan, in his robotic form, calculated their movements and found ways to outsmart

Ravok's minions. Jax and Nina fought fiercely alongside them, their weapons flashing in the dim light.

After what felt like hours of battling, they finally reached the heart of the fortress—Ravok's throne room. The dark sorcerer himself stood before them, his eyes filled with malice.

"You're too late," Ravok sneered. "The Heartstones are mine, and with them, I will bring an end to the Tree of Life."

Tara stepped forward, holding the golden Heartstone high. "Not if we stop you first," she said, her voice steady but filled with determination.

With a final surge of power, Tara and Leo activated the Heartstones. The golden Heartstone radiated light, while the red Heartstone crackled with destructive energy. Together, the two Heartstones unleashed a wave of power that shook the entire fortress.

Ravok roared in fury, but it was too late. The combined forces of the Heartstones overwhelmed him, trapping him in a cage of light and power. His dark magic began to unravel as the energy of the Heartstones consumed him.

The End of Ravok

With a final scream, Ravok vanished, his body disintegrating into the light. The fortress shook, its walls crumbling as the Heartstones continued to pulse with energy. Tara, Leo, and the rest of the group stood in the center of the chaos, their hearts racing but their spirits unbroken.

"We did it," Tara whispered, her voice filled with awe.

Leo nodded, a smile tugging at the corner of his lips. "Together."

The Heartstones safe in their hands, their power spent. Tara felt a sense of peace wash over her as the Tree of Life's energy surged around them, healing the damage caused by Ravok's dark magic.

With Ravok defeated and the Tree of Life safe, the group stood together, ready for whatever came next.

XVI

The Legacy of the Tree

The sun rose over the horizon, casting a soft golden glow across the land. The team stood at the edge of Ravok's crumbled fortress, the remnants of his dark stronghold now scattered across the landscape. The Heartstones in their hands had faded, their power spent after the battle. But a sense of calm had replaced the chaos that once reigned here.

Tara looked around at her friends. They had come so far, endured so much, and defeated Ravok. Yet, the journey didn't feel complete. The power of the Heartstones had faded, but something told her that their mission was far from over. The Tree of Life still held secrets, and they had yet to uncover them.

"We did it," Leo said quietly, looking around at the ruins of Ravok's fortress. "But I feel like there's something we're missing. Something more we need to do."

Tara nodded, her fingers still gripping the golden Heartstone, though its glow had diminished. "I feel it too. We didn't just come here to stop Ravok. There's something about the Tree of Life that we haven't yet understood."

Oakheart's words echoed in her mind. "The Heartstones are part of something greater, something that must be protected for all of time." She glanced at the others, knowing they shared her thoughts.

Ethan, who had switched back to his human form after the battle, looked up at the sky. "We may have stopped Ravok, but the Tree still needs us. The Heartstones might be gone, but the balance of life and death is delicate. We can't let that balance slip."

Jax, who had been quiet for a while, stepped forward. "What if the Heartstones were just the beginning? What if the Tree has other secrets, ones we're supposed to protect?"

Leo frowned. "So, you're saying the fight isn't over? That there are more enemies?"

Jax nodded. "It's possible. And maybe that's why we were chosen—to protect it for good. But if we don't understand the Tree fully, we could be walking into even more danger."

Tara turned to Oakheart, who had been watching them silently. His calm presence was reassuring, but his eyes held the weight of knowledge. "Oakheart," Tara asked, "Is there more to the Tree of Life? Something we need to know?"

Oakheart studied them for a moment before speaking. "There is much about the Tree that has been hidden for centuries. But it is not a secret that can be unlocked easily. The Heartstones were part of the Tree's protection, but they are not the only means of safeguarding it."

"Then what else is there?" Leo asked.

Oakheart's gaze softened. "The Tree of Life is more than just a source of power—it is a living being. It is connected to every living creature on this planet. The Heartstones may have been its most visible guardians, but the Tree's true protection lies in the hearts of those who are chosen to protect it."

Tara felt a deep sense of understanding. "So, it's not just about the Heartstones. It's about us—about our bond with the Tree."

Oakheart nodded. "Exactly. The Tree's power is not something that can be controlled or contained. It must be protected by those who are worthy, by those who understand the true balance of life and death."

"But what does that mean for us?" Jax asked.

Oakheart smiled gently. "It means you must continue your journey. You have proven yourselves by defeating Ravok, but now you must go further. You must learn the deeper truths about the Tree and the balance it holds."

Tara's mind raced. "What do we need to do?"

"First," Oakheart said, "you must return to the Tree of Life. The Heartstones have lost their power, but the Tree's connection to the world remains strong. You must seek out the ancient temple hidden deep within the forest. There, you will find the answers you seek."

Tara exchanged glances with the others. It was clear that their mission wasn't over. They still had more to learn, more to protect. They couldn't stop until the Tree of Life was fully safeguarded.

The Journey to the Temple

The team set out the next day, traveling toward the heart of the forest. The journey was long and arduous, but they were no longer afraid. They had fought battles, faced dark magic, and stood together as a team. Nothing could stop them now.

As they walked through the dense forest, Tara felt the presence of the Tree of Life growing stronger. It called to them, its energy reaching out, guiding them toward the hidden temple. The trees seemed to part for them, and the air grew thick with magic. They were getting closer.

After hours of walking, they finally arrived at the entrance of the temple. It was unlike anything they had ever seen—a massive structure made of stone, covered in vines and ancient symbols. The door was carved with intricate patterns that seemed to pulse with energy, as if alive.

"This is it," Ethan said, his voice filled with awe.

Leo stepped forward, his hand resting on the door. "It's strange," he said softly. "I feel like I've been here before."

Tara turned to him. "What do you mean?"

Leo shook his head. "I'm not sure. It's just a feeling. But I think we're meant to be here."

Jax nodded. "It's like the Tree is calling us, telling us we need to enter."

They pushed open the door, and the air inside the temple was thick with the power of the Tree. It felt ancient and wise, as if the very walls held the secrets of the world.

At the center of the temple was a large stone pedestal, and on it lay a glowing orb. The orb pulsed with energy, sending waves of light through the room. It was beautiful, but Tara could feel its power—raw, untamed, and dangerous.

"This is it," Oakheart's voice echoed in their minds. "The heart of the Tree. The orb holds the knowledge you seek."

Tara stepped forward cautiously, her fingers brushing against the orb. As she touched it, a vision filled her mind. She saw the Tree of Life, glowing with brilliant light, and felt its power flow through her. She saw the world connected to it—every living thing, every plant, every animal—its heartbeat echoing through the earth.

The vision shifted, and she saw Ravok again, his dark power trying to corrupt the Tree. The Heartstones had been created to protect the Tree, but they were not enough. The Tree needed something more—it needed the protectors to truly understand its power, to become one with it.

Tara pulled her hand back, breathless from the vision. "The Tree... it's not just about fighting. It's about understanding, protecting, and living in harmony with it."

Oakheart's voice echoed in her mind once more. "You are ready. The Tree has chosen you. You have proven your strength, your bond, and your love for the world. The journey does not end here. You will carry the Tree's wisdom and power within you."

Tara looked at the others, her heart swelling with pride and determination. "We will protect the Tree. We will protect the world."

The Final Test

As the team stood in the temple, the air around them began to tremble with energy. Tara looked toward the door, sensing that something was coming. Suddenly, the ground beneath them shook violently, and a deep, rumbling voice filled the room.

"You think you have won, protectors of the Tree?" The voice was dark and familiar. "This is not over."

Ravok's shadowy form materialized before them, his eyes glowing with hatred. But something was different. He no longer had the Heartstones, and his power seemed diminished. Still, the malevolent aura around him made Tara's heart race.

"You should not have come here," Ravok sneered. "The Tree of Life will fall. I will make sure of it."

Before they could react, Ravok reached out with a wave of his hand, sending a shockwave of dark energy toward them. The force was powerful, but it wasn't enough to stop them. Tara and the others stood firm, their connection to the Tree of Life protecting them.

With a roar of fury, Ravok began to retreat, but not before unleashing one final, destructive blast. The blast hit the ground, and with a tremendous explosion, Ravok was trapped beneath the roots of the Tree, his body ensnared in an ancient magic that pulled him into the earth.

Tara gasped. "He's trapped!"

"Yes," Oakheart's voice came from within the temple. "The Tree has claimed him. He is now bound to the earth, his power sealed."

"But he's not dead," Jax said, his voice filled with concern. "He's just... trapped."

Oakheart's voice was solemn. "Ravok's fate is not death. He will remain beneath the Tree, his power sealed for now. But remember, evil never truly dies. The Tree of Life is a living being—it will protect itself, but it will also watch over Ravok. And if he ever returns, you must be ready."

Tara turned to her friends, determination in her heart. "We will be ready. We will protect the Tree, no matter what."

Together, they stood at the heart of the Tree of Life, ready to face whatever came next. Their journey wasn't over. It had only just begun.

XVII

The Whisper of the
Future

The night was quiet, but the air was thick with an unspoken tension. The team stood at the edge of the Tree of Life, their faces illuminated by the soft, ethereal glow of its vast branches. The world around them seemed to hold its breath, as if waiting for something to happen. After everything they had endured, the peace they had fought for felt fragile, like a delicate thread hanging in the balance.

Tara looked up at the Tree, her fingers still clasping the Heartstone, now dull but pulsing softly with an inner rhythm. She could still feel its presence deep within her, the connection between her and the Tree of Life. The vision she had experienced in the temple lingered in her mind, the whispers of the Tree still echoing in her ears.

"It's quiet," Leo said, his voice breaking the silence. He was standing beside her, his gaze fixed on the Tree. "Too quiet. It almost feels like it's waiting for something."

Tara nodded. "It's the calm before the storm, I think. I can feel it too. The Tree is strong, but I don't think the battle is truly over."

Jax, who had been standing silently a little further away, stepped forward. His eyes were sharp, scanning the horizon. "Ravok may be trapped, but there's more to this. The power we've unlocked—there's still so much we don't understand."

Ethan, still in his human form, stood next to Jax, arms crossed. "You're right. We've only scratched the surface. Oakheart told us there's more to the Tree than we know. But it doesn't feel like Ravok was the only threat."

Tara turned toward Ethan. "You think there's something else out there, something worse than Ravok?"

"I don't know," Ethan said quietly. "But I feel like the Tree is trying to tell us something. Something we're not seeing yet."

The night grew colder, and the wind picked up, rustling the leaves of the Tree. The once peaceful air now carried a sense of urgency. Tara's heart raced, her instincts warning her that something was coming. Something that could change everything.

Suddenly, a deep, reverberating hum echoed from within the Tree. It was low at first, like a heartbeat, but it grew louder, shaking the ground beneath their feet. The light around the Tree began to pulse erratically, casting strange shadows across the land. It was as though the Tree itself was reacting to something—something hidden, something waiting.

"Do you feel that?" Tara whispered, her voice trembling.

Before anyone could answer, a blinding light erupted from the center of the Tree, illuminating the entire forest. The light was not warm, but cold, as if it were a warning.

Tara shielded her eyes, her heart pounding in her chest.

And then, just as suddenly as it had appeared, the light vanished.

The silence that followed was deafening.

"What was that?" Jax asked, his voice low with a mixture of confusion and fear.

"I don't know," Tara replied, her voice barely a whisper. "But I feel like we've awakened something."

Ethan took a step back, his tech-savvy mind racing. "That wasn't just a random event. The Tree is reacting to something, and I don't think it's a good sign."

Leo glanced at Tara, his eyes serious. "Tara, do you think it's connected to Ravok? Or something else entirely?"

Tara bit her lip, uncertainty clouding her thoughts. "I don't know. But I have a bad feeling. It's like the Tree has been holding something back... something powerful."

A distant rumble echoed across the sky, and the ground beneath their feet trembled once more. It was faint at first, but growing louder, as if something was stirring deep within the earth. Tara's heart skipped a beat as she glanced around, looking for any sign of danger.

"We need to get out of here," Leo said urgently, his voice filled with concern. "The Tree... it's warning us."

But before anyone could move, the air was filled with a strange, melodic sound—a song that seemed to come from the very heart of the Tree. It wasn't a song anyone had heard before, but it was hauntingly beautiful, pulling them toward the center of the Tree as if it were calling them.

The team stood frozen, entranced by the music, unsure of whether to approach or retreat. Tara's mind raced, trying to understand what was happening. The light, the rumble, the song—everything pointed to something far more ancient than they had anticipated.

Ethan stepped forward, his eyes scanning the area. "This... this is bigger than we thought. The Tree is trying to communicate with us."

"But what is it saying?" Tara asked, barely able to hear her own voice over the song that filled the air.

Before anyone could respond, the ground shook violently. The roots of the Tree seemed to shift and move, as if something beneath it was awakening. The team jumped back, their eyes wide with shock.

"Get back!" Jax shouted, grabbing Tara's arm and pulling her away from the roots. "Something's wrong! Something's coming!"

Tara stumbled back, her heart racing. The song had stopped, but the ground still trembled beneath them. It was as though the very earth was alive, reacting to the power below. She could feel the pressure building, a force pulling at her very soul.

Suddenly, a crack split the ground near the Tree, sending a shockwave through the forest. The team watched in horror as a dark figure began to rise from the crack, emerging from deep within the earth. It was tall and shadowy, its features obscured by the swirling darkness that surrounded it. But one thing was clear—it was not a force they had faced before.

Tara's breath caught in her throat as she stared at the figure. This wasn't Ravok. It was something far older, far more dangerous.

"Who... what is that?" Leo whispered, his voice filled with awe and terror.

Tara didn't have an answer. All she knew was that they were facing something that was not from this world.

Before anyone could react, the figure's eyes glowed with a cold, malevolent light. It opened its mouth, and a voice that seemed to echo from the depths of time itself filled the air.

"You think you've won?" the voice boomed, sending chills down Tara's spine. "You are merely pawns in a game much larger than you can comprehend. The Tree is not just a protector. It is a gateway—a doorway to a power beyond your control."

Tara's heart raced as the ground trembled once again. This was not the end. It was only the beginning.

And then, just as quickly as the figure had appeared, it vanished back into the earth, leaving the team standing in stunned silence.

"Get ready," Jax said, his voice grim. "We haven't seen the last of this."

Tara's thoughts raced. What was that thing? And what did it mean for the future of the Tree of Life?

The answer, she knew, was still out of reach.

But the storm was coming.

And they would have to face it—together.

To be continued...

www.ingramcontent.com/pod-product-compliance
Lightning Source LLC
Chambersburg PA
CBHW062223150726
47991CB00006B/2408